P9-DER-160

THE KINGDOM WITHIN

Mystic Harbor
PRESS

Copyright © 2014 Mystic Harbor Press,
an imprint of Smooth Sailing Press, LLC
www.smoothsailingpress.com
www.thekingdomwithinseries.com

No part of this publication may be reproduced, distributed or trans-
mitted in any form or by any means (electronic, mechanical, photo-
copied, recorded or otherwise), without the written permission of
Smooth Sailing Press, LLC.

ISBN: 978-1-61899-063-1 (Special Edition Hardcover)
ISBN: 978-1-61899-052-5 (Paperback)
ISBN: 978-1-61899-053-2 (eBook)

Publishers Note: The Kingdom Within is a work of fiction.
Characters, names, places and incidents are either the author's
imagination or are used fictitiously, and any resemblance to an
actual persons, living or dead, business establishments, events or
locations is entirely coincidental.

to ELLENY ♡

K<small>The</small>INGDOM WITHIN

BY

SAMANTHA GILLESPIE

To my sister, for always believing in me.

Prologue

"Their fear is your weapon." The old man's words ring loud and true within the walls of the banquet room. They display eloquently against the pale face of his latest target—or rather, his latest conquest. The rebellious nature of the fugitive landowner before him crumbled to an embarrassing spectacle of soiled trousers and desperate pleas.

"I'll pay double," he says through hasty breaths.

The old man smiles. "Your debt is no longer a concern." He gestures to the two armored men who hold the landowner captive. "Guards, please introduce him to Eva." The landowner throws nervous glances at the guards as they usher him across the room. Like all the others before him, it takes him a moment to realize who Eva is. I watch him stiffen, throwing his legs out in front of him to stall the guards, his heels dragging uselessly against the polished wood. He gives in to a series of screams as they reach the human shaped cabinet. It stands open, the long, sharp internal spikes ready to impale its next victim.

"Life is a cradle of victories and failures, my son," the old man says over the man's screams, raising his cup to me. "The more victorious you are—"

"The longer I shall live," I finish flatly. "I can recite your teachings in my sleep, old man. When will I get to do anything with them?"

He takes his time to answer, enjoying the last of the land-owner's melody as Eva's iron door grinds to a close. He welcomes the ensuing silence with a sigh. "You are young still, boy. But if you are ever to do my bidding, you must work on your patience; revenge is not to be rushed."

I snort. "What is it now, thirty years? I'd wager you are in no danger of rushing anything." The old man stares back through zealous eyes.

"Patience, son. The best poison is that which spreads through unsuspecting veins, killing slowly and gradually. The kind that tastes sweet to the tongue and doesn't bitter until the very end."

Chapter One

Flames engulf the hall. They scorch a path of destruction, consuming the space around me. Thick, black smoke clouds my view, disorienting me. I press on blindly anyway. I could be headed for a dead end and imminent death, but what choice do I have? I can't just stand here.

I'm desperate for a breath of fresh air. The raw irritation in my throat forces me to cough so violently I can't move. I rest a hand against the fevered wall as I try to regain composure. Lungs burning, I inhale but only swallow more smoke.

Then, out of the corner of my eye, I see a faint light. I hold my breath and run toward it. A sense of relief spreads in my aching chest and I will myself to move faster. As I get closer, I can make out the hazy shape of a window. I force my legs to keep running and ignore the suffocating feeling that chokes me and screams at me to slow down. I grip the window's blackened frame and shove my head and torso outside. I gasp, relieved to inhale something other than smoke. When I look down, however, my hopes of survival are instantly crushed. The ground is too far. If I jump, I will die. Panic washes through me. For a moment, I'm rooted to the window, unable to make a decision. No matter what I do, I'm going to die. But then I feel the heat behind me, closer and stronger with each second. In my mind, I picture jumping to my death. I tell myself that I can do it, that I'd rather break every bone in my body than burn. Perhaps, if I'm lucky, I won't feel any pain. I close my eyes and jump. Tightening my muscles, I brace for impact. But nothing happens. I don't feel myself falling, nor do I feel the gushing rush of air at my descent. I feel nothing. Am I dead? Maybe falling to my death was a painless way to go after all.

A mocking laugh erupts nearby. Confused, I open my eyes. I'm on the ground. A man towers before me, the sun shining brightly above him, casting a shadow over his face. I hold a hand to my eyes and squint. I don't know what he looks like but somehow I know. King Theros. The cruel king who takes lives and land mercilessly without remorse. At his side, he holds a long sword that drips with the dark red of fresh blood.

Is that my blood? My dress is intact; the fall hasn't even ripped the fabric. When I look up again, I register countless bodies in pools of blood, scattered across the courtyard, beyond the gates and the outskirts of the palace. My eyes continue down the silent path of terror, finally resting at its point of origin, the town below. Or what is left of it. It is the living depiction of chaos, a painting, brushed on its canvas with vicious strokes. I hear the distant cries of men, women, and children, the slashing of swords, the crackling of buildings burning, and the undeniable thunder of cannons. Nauseous, I turn away from the violent scene, just in time to see King Theros raise his sword and thrust it into my chest.

I wake up gasping, hands clutching at my chest. I am drenched in sweat.

"My lady?"

I look up to see Anabella, my chambermaid, running up to me; in her arms is a pile of folded clothes.

"I'm all right," I mumble. "I was having a nightmare."

"Well, that was some nightmare, child; you are sweating like a pig."

She pulls back the covers, exposing my bare legs to the chill of the room. "You need to get ready. The king's expecting you."

I frown. What does he want now? Every time Father wishes

an audience, it's because I did something inexcusable, or because there are important matters to discuss. Matters that have to do with me, that is. Anything and everything else is apparently none of my business. I sigh. I am probably being scolded, but for what, I haven't the faintest idea.

I get into the tub and shiver in the cold water. I don't bother complaining to Anabella. I'm happy enough that she has agreed to let me bathe on my own. I have always hated the idea of having others wait on me, tending to my every wish and command as if I were too useless to do anything on my own. Fortunately, I've never had to deal with ladies in waiting. Though it's a widely practiced royal tradition, Father never assigned me any. He's always believed that a chambermaid is more than enough for me, though I am pretty sure his reasoning has something to do with my unruly nature. I am too crude, too clumsy to have more delicate companions.

But I am fortunate to have Anabella. A woman wise beyond her gray hairs, she is the queen of cleanliness and tidiness, and the epitome of multitasking; I've been in her care since I was a little girl. She is like the mother I never knew. My mother, Queen Olivia, died several months after I was born. She fell ill with a mysterious fever that physicians had no cure for. They tried many things—ointments, herbs, rituals, leeches, bloodletting, prayers. None of it worked, and her health quickly deteriorated. That is all I know of her. Father seldom mentions her, but thanks to the portrait that hangs in his study, I at least know what she looked like. A lot like me, it seems. I inherited her golden locks and tender amber eyes. Father once said he could almost see her looking out through my eyes. I wish I knew what she was like, not as others knew her, but as a daughter would know a mother. Thinking of her brings forth an odd feeling of emptiness, like a part of me is missing.

Anabella helps me into my dress.

"What was it about? Your nightmare?" she asks while she ties my corset. A chill runs down my arms at the recollection.

"The same I always have—Stonefall's defeat to King Theros."

"Oh," she replies.

"This time I died by his sword."

I touch my chest instinctively. My dreams have tormented me with Stonefall's demise many times now. I die a different way every time, but the nightmare always ends in the slaughter of my people. Anabella shakes her head, pressing her palm against the creases of my dress.

"You need to stop having those dreams before they come true."

"They will never come true," I counter, as if it were a fact written in stone. "Theros would not dare attack Stonefall once the alliance with Alder is solidified. He might be powerful, but he is no fool."

It's tragic really, that the fate of a kingdom rests on me. I've never been in love and yet I've been betrothed from the moment I filled my lungs with air. I am to be married when I turn eighteen, which is a little less than a year from now. The marriage was arranged by my parents and the king and queen of Alder, my future in-laws and the leaders of the most powerful kingdom in the Eastern Continent. My stomach stirs uneasily at the thought. I have never met the prince nor seen a portrait of him, though I have overheard many people at court comment that he is rumored to be quite charming. Still, I can't help but be terrified at the prospect of marrying a complete stranger.

When I was first told my fate, I decided to run away. I would never let my father do such a thing to me. That was, of course, before the alliance between Stonefall and Alder weakened. Father never spoke a word to me about it, and I didn't ask any questions. Perhaps, I thought, I would not have to marry the prince after all. But my joy was short lived. When news of the waning alliance reached the kingdom of Talos, King Theros immediately set his greedy sights on our kingdom. Theros' thirst for power and control was insatiable. His own father had embarked on a mission to overthrow the countries of the Western Continent, a land of famine and poverty, ready for the taking. But he was stopped short by a plague that killed thousands, the king of Talos included. The continent was quarantined, and Theros rose to power. No one was surprised he was interested in a vulnerable kingdom like Stonefall. With lush, rolling hills and flowing rivers, it's the most beautiful kingdom in the Eastern Continent. It also happens to be one of the smallest; our army is almost pitiful in size. Our army has many courageous and honorable soldiers who would die for their kingdom without question, but I do not want to sacrifice them. As much as I dislike the prospect of marrying a complete stranger, if it keeps our soldiers alive and our kingdoms intact, I know it is the right thing to do.

My shoes resound against the empty hallway. The noise disturbs the deep silence and echoes against the marble columns and stucco walls. A light breeze dances with the translucent curtains that hang from the floor-to-ceiling windows. I can see the courtyard through them. An intricate maze of geometrically trimmed bushes decorates the walkways around a large fountain. Beyond the courtyard is my favorite area of the palace, an enchanting grove of old oak trees, where I can practically spend an entire day without being bothered. The court is not too fond of nature. They seem to prefer the courtyard, where they congregate to socialize and gossip.

Outside Father's study, the door ward opens the heavy wooden doors. They groan against their hinges as they swing open into the small chamber. I can't imagine what I have done wrong this time. I've been on my best behavior lately, all serene smiles and repressed opinions. And all to please him. If I am a better daughter, then Father might learn to love me, if only a little. I used to think he particularly disliked me, but I know now he's simply hardhearted. He places great trust in his closest friends and advisers, but never offers a hint of warmth, not even for my uncle, the Duke of Elsham.

I take a deep breath and step inside. Greeted with the pungent scent of burning candles and leather-bound books, I keep my head down as I walk. I do not dare look at Father, expecting a fierce glare. But when I hear nothing from him, save for papers rummaging, I bite my lip and lift my gaze.

Hunched over a desk blanketed by documents, Father studies what looks to be a letter. A lock of gray hair hangs out of place, dangling across his forehead. With a rich, red robe, and large gold rings adorning several of his fingers, he looks indeed like a king. I realize he must be ignoring me. Surely he heard me come in. He seems agitated.

"Father?" I croak.

He drops the piece of paper in his hands and looks up at me. To my surprise, there is no anger in his eyes. So accustomed to his disapproval, I find its absence a little disconcerting.

"Meredith," he says, clearing his throat. "Sit down." He motions at the chair in front of his desk. The empty seat beckons like an omen. I move quietly, though I'm sure the sudden, nervous pounding in my chest is loud enough to hear. I have no idea what he is about to tell me, but from the lines on his face and the tightness around his eyes, I can tell it's serious.

"It has come to my attention that King Theros wants you dead," he says quickly, as if addressing his advisers on matters of state. I take the news with a hard swallow. The man who haunts my dreams wants to kill me. Are my nightmares premonitions? I feel the room spin as a heavy weight creeps into my chest, making it hard to breathe. "It seems Theros will go to any lengths to prevent your marriage to the prince of Alder. Thus, I've hired an escort to help keep you safe. He is to remain at your side at all functions and anytime you step foot outside the palace walls. Is that clear?" He speaks so fast that it takes me a moment to register every word.

I want to ask him a dozen questions. Who is he? Where is he from? Can he be trusted? But Father is not fond of being questioned, so I manage to hold my tongue and simply nod.

I look up at the wall behind him, at my mother's portrait, hoping to find some comfort, some reassurance that everything will be all right. I hate that I can see her only in his study. I insisted many times that her portrait be hung by the main hall— what better face to welcome visitors? Father never approved; he wants her all to himself.

"Meredith," Father says, redirecting my thoughts.

"Yes, Father?"

"Do you understand the seriousness of this matter? You must never leave his sight; your life may very well depend on it." He questions me with a raised brow. An unsettling feeling burrows deeply into my stomach.

"I understand. When will this escort arrive?"

"Soon. You may go now."

Just like that, he dismisses me, making no effort to set my mind at ease. I sit there, slack-jawed and confused. If Father is indeed worried, does that not mean he cares? He does not wait for me to leave before returning to his work. And I realize it's not me he cares about. It's what would happen to our kingdom if I died that scares him.

"Oh and Meredith?" he says. "I expect to see you at the tournament."

I had forgotten. Today is opening day for the jousting tournament. A silent groan churns in my throat. I am in no mood to endure such a social event. Last year, I made it a point to miss it.

Chapter Two

A pleasing aroma of garlic and herbs infuses the narrow, low-ceilinged hallway that branches into several chambers. The kitchen bubbles with life, cooks bustling and servants going about their daily routines. I should be on my way to the tournament, but I figured I could make a quick stop at the bake house to visit with Beth first. Squeezing through, I navigate around the servants through the hall that connects the pantry to the bake house. The warm, comforting smell of fresh baked bread welcomes me to the pint-sized room. A trace of apples and cinnamon lingers by the oven next to the open window. Pots, pans, rolling pins, and baskets litter the worktables, and there is no surface that isn't covered in flour.

Beth works at the back, on a small corner table, mashing dough with her knuckles more vigorously than usual. After spending the entire morning soothing Anabella's anxiety, and dealing with my own, I desperately need my friend. Beth, unlike Anabella, is someone I actually want to confide in, someone with whom I can share my fears and sorrows without having to worry about her suffering a stroke.

"Smells like apple pie," I chirp. Beth breaks away from her work, startled. Sprinkles of flour cover her nose and cheeks.

"Oh, hi Mer. What brings you down here so early?" Beth and I met as children. Her aunt Esther, the baker, brought her to the palace to escape her father's beatings at home. Fond of exploring, I'd spied on her a couple of times in the grove, where she would wander off with a small basket to collect flowers. Beth would stroll around the trees and bushes until her basket was full. Spending time with the other kids at court, I quickly realized I was different. For the sake of having friends, I tried my best to be interested in dolls and dancing. Given my two left feet, dancing was nearly impossible. And dolls, well, there was only so much pretend I could play before losing interest. My suggestion of an adventurous doll who lived in the woods was received with funny looks and silence. Before long, I was out in the grove, playing pretend on my own, chasing imaginary monsters with sticks, digging holes and making mud pies. There was not a single day I did not go back inside without a completely soiled dress.

It took me a few days to approach Beth, mainly because I knew I wasn't allowed to play with servants, but also because deep down I thought she would think me different too. I couldn't bear to be rejected again. But then, one day, a flower fell out of her basket.

"Wait. You dropped this," I said, holding out the delicate purple flower. A little alarmed, Beth hesitantly took it before running off into the courtyard. The next time I was prepared with a basket of my own. "Mind if I join you?" I asked. She responded with a wordless nod. She wouldn't speak unless I asked her something, so at first, I had to ask a lot of questions. Eventually though, she warmed up to me. Soon enough, we were running around and making mud pies together. Members of the staff looked at us through wary eyes and nervous glances, unsure of how to handle the hoyden princess that roamed their kitchen, chasing after a servant girl. It was only a matter of time before the attention faded. The other children of the staff, too, became accustomed to my presence, but would keep their distance, instructed by their parents that they were not to mingle with royalty. Save for one boy. Of all of children, Holt was the only one who dared to spend time with Beth and me, that is, whenever his mother was too preoccupied to notice.

I dust off the flour from an empty stool and sit, letting my shoulders sag with the invisible weight they now carry. Beth tucks loose strands of her chocolate-brown hair away from her petite, round face.

"Is something wrong?" she asks, a hint of alarm in her otherwise carefree voice. Briefly, I recount the meeting with Father earlier this morning. I make sure to keep my voice steady. Beth's eyes widen. She wipes her hands on her apron and walks up to me. "Maker. Those are dreadful news, Mer."

I nod. I want to say that it's not as serious as it sounds, that nothing will come of it and everything will be just fine. And that might be true, but the hard lump in my throat tells me otherwise.

Beth sighs. "If it's any consolation, I've got problems of my own," she announces with a halfhearted smile.

That manages to distract me from the dread tingling in my chest. "What do you mean?"

Beth's lips press together in a slight grimace. "It's my mother," she says, slowly, almost in a whisper. She pauses and casts her eyes down. When she looks up at me, they are brimming with tears. "She's dying, Mer," she says, her voice breaking.

I sit there, shocked. Her mother is dying. It sounds surreal, as if that sort of thing doesn't really happen. How does someone cope with that? My own mother is dead, but I never experienced her loss, only her absence.

"Oh Beth, I am so sorry." I hold her, stroking her back as she gives in to her grief and sobs. "Is there anything I can do?" I ask when she pulls away. She wipes at her puffy eyes and shakes her head.

"I'm afraid there's nothing to be done. She is very ill. Esther says it might be a matter of days before..." she trails off, unable to say the words.

"How long have you known of her condition?"

"I learned of it only yesterday afternoon. Esther was quite reluctant to tell me, afraid that I would go see her and run into my father. But now, with no hope of recovery, she felt obliged to share the news." Beneath her sorrow, I hear the anger in her voice.

"You cannot go home alone, Beth," I remind her. "You don't know how your father will react. He might hurt you." I see a flicker of fear in her dark brown eyes.

"Esther will accompany me," she says, and the concern oozes out of my muscles.

"Perhaps I could accompany you as well," I say, biting my lip. "I could sneak out—"

"Please don't trouble yourself, Mer," she interjects. I shake my head.

"It's no trouble at all. You're my best friend. I would do anything for you, you know that." A small, grateful smile spreads across her face.

"I do, and I thank you for it. But it isn't safe for you to venture out, especially now."

"I suppose that does present a problem," I say, lightheartedly. We share a chuckle, despite the seriousness of our dilemmas.

"Good morning ladies." Holt prances in with a smile. I return the smile with some surprise. These days, running into Holt is about as likely as being struck by lightning; managing the constant need of wine from the members of court keeps him quite busy.

"It's a bit early to be staining your shirt, don't you think?" I ask him, gesturing at the purple splashes of wine on his sleeves. He gives me a toothy grin.

"Not as long as I get to take a few samples; drinking is a timeless art, you see."

"Careful now, Beth might take you for a drunk," I tease. From behind me, I hear Beth snort.

He gives me a look of theatrical incredulity. "We both know she is far too nice to think that of me."

"But do tell us Holt, besides your great desire to see us, what possessed you to come down here at this hour?" I ask.

"I just happened to be around the kitchen when I heard you two birds chirping away. I really should get back to work though, days like these come with a full plate."

"You shouldn't make the butler wait on you, he'll be angry," Beth warns in her gentle, motherly way.

Days like these? Suddenly, I remember where I'm supposed to be. "I have to go. Tournament duty," I say, making a face. Beth smiles.

"Have fun," she says, a little too enthusiastic.

I roll my eyes, giving Holt's shoulder a good-bye squeeze and dash out of the bake house, but then duck back in.

"Beth, please be careful."

Holt frowns in confusion, glancing at Beth, then at me. I answer with a pointed chin in Beth's direction. *Ask her.*

"Don't worry. I'll be fine."

With three guards in tow, I make my way to the tournament grandstands. Though still within palace grounds, the jousting arena lies outside the palace gates. Before today, I would have gladly avoided the stiff company of the guards, as I find it unnecessary and even a little silly. Today, however, I feel relieved by their presence and the swords at their belts, in spite of the detached demeanors. The guards are fully garbed in metal, with the Stonefall crest of an eagle engraved on their breastplates. The kingdom's colors show on the red cape draped across their torso, folded across the shoulder to show the white of the cape's underside.

The tournament is strategically held at high noon to provide the best light of day, with the sun at its highest point. The crowd sounds excited, cheering and whistling. Brightly colored pavilions surround the arena, where contestants prepare to joust. Walking up the wooden steps, I head to the center of the main grandstand, where a red canopy shades eight seats reserved for the king, the duke and his family, the king's advisers, and myself. I notice, slightly mortified, that there is only one empty seat left. I feel Father's glare as I take a seat at the opposite end of his row. I keep my eyes down to avoid his silent disapproval. But then a warm, strong hand reaches for mine and gives it a gentle squeeze. I smile knowingly and look up.

"My dear cousin," says Charles, flashing me with his signature dimpled smile. "It is so very good to see you."

I squeeze his hand in return. "Tell me Charles, who was the gracious soul that allowed me to sit next to you today?"

"You are looking at him," he says, with a serious tone and laughing eyes.

Charles is the embodiment of what every man ought to be: handsome, charming, sensible, generous, and affectionate. Above all, he is kind. I could live a thousand years and never meet another soul quite like him. He is nothing like his family. To this day, I find it hard to believe they are related, even with their strikingly similar features—fair, blond, and blue-eyed—save for the duchess. Charles's father, the Duke of Elsham, is not as severe as the king, and sometimes even shows gestures of affection to his family, but he is nevertheless a very somber man, one whose presence demands respect. Personally, I think he's a little creepy, though he pales in comparison to his wife. The duchess is a witch. Everything about her screams darkness. Her clothes are devoid of color, and her dark eyes and hair don't help either. I wouldn't be surprised if one day she started chanting in a mysterious tongue and turned us all into chickens. Their daughter, Charlotte, is by far the worst of them. As beautiful as she is vile, Charlotte is the bane of my existence. If there is one thing I look forward to in my marriage, it's getting away from her. How Charles manages to remain so agreeable despite having such a family can only be a testament to the strength of his character. I don't know how he does it. I cannot imagine living one week with them before losing my mind.

From behind, Charlotte whispers in my ear. "You reek of peasant, cousin." My pulse quickens. I turn, forcing the sour curl of my lips into a smile. She beams through her long lashes with venomous sweetness, an impish gleam sparkling in her blue eyes. At arm's reach, I can smell her usual scent of roses.

"I made sure to roll in the dirt with the pigs just for you," I say, with a playful wink.

When Charles opens his mouth to voice his objection to

Charlotte's behavior, I lightly rest my palm on his shoulder, shaking my head at him. It's pointless. Charles censures her every time he can, but it makes no difference to her. She will never give up. I honestly can't understand why. In the past, I have tried several times to patch things up, to bridge that invisible, incomprehensible gap that separates us, but it's been nothing but wasted effort. I have come to accept that there is nothing I can say or do to make her like me. Not that I want her to. She isn't exactly good friend material. But if you have a thorn in your shoe, the obvious choice is to try to remove it, or at the very least make it less...prickly.

Thankfully, before Charlotte can launch another barb at me, the trumpets blare, demanding our attention. The tournament's opening day is about to begin. With the roll of the drums, the judges ride in formal procession, one by one, stiffly seated on their horses. There's only a handful of them so it's not long before the contestants follow suit in similar form. Though there are a few foreigners participating, the contestants are primarily nobility and high-ranking officers. The crowd goes wild when Elijah Gannon, the kingdom's favorite noble, enters the arena. Elijah came to Stonefall four years ago. A foreigner with sharp good looks, and heir to a large fortune, he took the court by storm in a matter of months. Sought after by the ladies and admired by his peers, he is quite the popular figure. And, as if this is not enough, he decided to enter the jousting tournament on a whim. He took champion his first year. This will be his third year competing. I hate to admit that I'm impressed. I would never tell him so, of course. Elijah is as arrogant as they come, and something about him does not feel right to me, like that uncanny sensation when you think someone is watching you. Out of the corner of my eye, I see a group of ladies fawning over him. They swoon and giggle, and wave their handkerchiefs in his direction.

"What do you think, cousin, will Elijah win again this year?" Charles whispers, leaning into my ear.

"I pray that he doesn't. He is the last person in the world I want to dance with." The winner of the tournament is entitled to a large purse, along with the armor and horses of his defeated opponents. But as this is my last year as an unmarried lady, this year's victor will also be granted the opening dance at the summer court ball, as my partner.

"He is not so bad once you get to know him," Charles says.

I snort. "Charles, you are too kind on the fellow. I know him well enough, and I don't like him. Not one bit."

"You're just jealous because he doesn't give you any attention," Charlotte scoffs. I almost contradict her. Elijah will gladly give his attention to any female within reach. To his credit, though, it seems to work well for him. Just not with me. But that doesn't stop him from trying.

"Charlotte, you know very well intruding on other people's conversations does not speak well of your manners," Charles mutters.

"Nor does frolicking with peasants," she retorts pointedly.

If only I could throw a fist at that pretty face of hers, send her flying backward with her feet rolling over her head. But my options are limited: respond with equal malice or remain silent. I prefer to not fuel her fire and go with the latter. All Charlotte wants is to rile me up, to get a response out of me. I will not give her the satisfaction.

Charles bristles. "Ignore her," I say. "It's easily done, believe me, I do it all the time."

He shakes his head, pinching his lips together. "How can I ever make amends for such behavior?" I clasp his hand firmly.

"Having you for a cousin is more than enough." And I mean it. Charles is the only relative who has ever shown me affection. I treasure him dearly. I would put up with a dozen Charlottes if I had to, just to have him in my life. His lips stretch into a genuine smile that lights up his face.

With the procession coming to an end, the contestants of the first round are announced in glamorous prose by their squires. I don't recognize the names, save for the few who have been competing for years. Contestants don't usually stick around for more than two seasons. Tournaments are brutal. They take a toll on the body. It's enough to deter most men.

At the blast of the trumpet, the dueling contestants charge forth on their horse, fully armored and ready to attack. With a measly beam of wood in between them, they gallop, lance in hand, ready to deal a blow of brute strength against their quickly approaching opponent. The duelers crash their lances into each other with a loud bang; wood splinters fly in all directions. I cringe instinctively, praying that no one is fatally wounded. It happens every so often, which is yet another reason I avoid attending these tournaments. Several years ago, witnessing a man fall off his horse and never get up changed me. Something deep inside crumbled, watching someone die like that for mere entertainment.

Thankfully, neither man is wounded. The joust proceeds to the second round. They carry on this way until one is successful at throwing the other off his horse, at which point they are congratulated by the audience with a wave of applause. Then the next two contestants take their turn, and they continue until they all have dueled. The judges, of course, leave the best duel for last. The crowd surges as Elijah steps up on his horse to face his opponent. A Sir Kobrick is the lucky one to face-off against him. I've not seen Sir Kobrick joust before. Does he stand a chance? I lean forward, struggling to get a good look at him. He appears to be a formidably sized foe, but his armor cloaks too much of him to be sure. The trumpet blares again, and they are off. I keep my fingers crossed, silently rooting for the mysterious Sir Kobrick. If Elijah loses his first match, he will be instantly out of the competition, and I will not have to worry about dancing with him anymore. Besides, a dose of failure would do him good.

But when the lances clash, Sir Kobrick is instantly thrown off his horse. The audience erupts into a jolting series of shouts, throwing victorious fists and waving arms. I realize I am sitting with my mouth hanging open. I shut it. Either Elijah is really good at his craft, or everyone else is really bad. Not that it matters. The idea of dancing with Elijah, of having him so close and touching me makes me cringe. But this is only the first day; he hasn't won yet. I silently pray for him to trip in a pothole.

The jousting ends and it's time to celebrate. Though at the moment, celebrating is the last thing I want to do. Music, drinking, and dancing await us at the courtyard. Not one for court gossip, I immediately attempt to retreat. But Charles, already expecting this, asks me to stay. "Just for a little while," I tell him.

He smiles, triumphant. "I'll take what I can." I'm about to suggest that we take a walk around the grove when Elijah shows up, a pretty girl clinging to his arm like she's a bee and he's the honey. His chiseled face, framed by loose, strawberry blond locks, wears the smug look of victory.

"Charles, my friend, I was wondering why you had not yet

given me your felicitations, but then I saw you in the company of our lovely princess and I quickly understood. It is a rare occurrence to be graced with your presence, your highness," Elijah says, resting his probing gaze on me. I throw a fake smile at him. Sensing my tension, Charles steers the conversation back to Elijah.

"I do owe you my congratulations. You played flawlessly."

"You were so wonderful," squeals the girl on Elijah's arm. And he soaks up the flattery like a sponge. I resist the urge to gag.

"Yes, well, you'll have to keep up the wonderful for an entire week if you are to win the tournament," Charles jokes.

Elijah's mouth curves up at the corner.

"Come now, Charles, are you suggesting I might lose?" Charles gives him a bemused smirk.

"Please excuse me," I say, abruptly. "There is a sour taste in my mouth I wish to rid myself of." Elijah cocks his head, his mouth twitching with amusement. Not waiting for Charles to object and convince me to stay, I hastily walk away, not looking back.

On my way to my rooms, Esther rushes toward me, her black, gray-streaked hair, always neatly combed into her cap, rumpled and unruly.

"Your highness!" she says through hasty breaths. I take in the alarmed gaze on her blanched face and the realization hits me before she can explain. Beth.

"Has she gone to see her mother?" I ask, my mouth dry.

"Yes." She nods bleakly." She left early this morning and hasn't returned."

"Why did you not accompany her?" Her brow draws in quizzically, deepening the wrinkles on her forehead.

"Accompany her? Your highness, I forbade her to go. She agreed she would not. If I had known what she was planning, I would have stopped her."

She lied to me, I realize.

A flush of disappointment whirls inside me. "Your highness, you must send the guards immediately!" I shake my head.

"I have no authority to do that. Such an order has to come from the king himself." Esther clasps my hands together.

"You don't understand; her father despises her for deserting her home." She swallows, looking me straight in the eye. "He will kill her." The chilling words turn my blood to ice. Kill her? Is her father that violent? Would he kill his own daughter?

I bite my lip, unsure of my options. "I will speak to my father, but I cannot guarantee his help. If he denies me, we'll have to go after her ourselves."

"No, your highness!" she says, hastily grasping my arm in a firm hold. "That will not do. We don't have the strength to stop that brute." I pull my arm away.

"So what do you suggest, then? Leave her to her fate?"

"It was her decision; she knew the risk." I balk at her apathy.

"Her mother is dying," I say with a clipped voice.

At this, her face darkens with grave intensity. She speaks very slowly. "I almost died by his hand once. I will not risk my life again so foolishly." I take a step back, disbelief slapping me in the face. How could she be so selfish?

"You will let your niece die to save your own skin? You should be ashamed of yourself," I mutter in disgust. Not wasting another second, I leave her to her cowardice. Beth is my best friend and she needs me. I will do whatever it takes to bring her back safely.

Chapter Three

I wait for Father in the privacy of my rooms, away from the eyes and ears of the court where I might have a chance, if any, at swaying his opinion. As I pace about the sitting room, my hands gripping the stiff boning of my bodice at my waist, a small thought invades my agitation. Will he even show? I made it very clear to the guard I sent to fetch him that it was an urgent matter. But will he listen? Father's tendency to disregard my requests is typical. My thoughts break as Father appears through my door, a company of guards flocking behind him. He scans around my room, eyebrows raised. "This had better be good."

I take a hard swallow. "I must speak with you alone."

"Leave us," he instructs his guards. The door settles into its frame with a gentle click. "Speak," he says at once, his voice carrying that imperious presence of his across the room. I resist the urge to perch my shaky legs on the couch.

"Father, I need your help," I stammer.

"With what?" he asks, his face impassive. My lungs fill with an unsteady breath. I knew this wasn't going to be easy. Still, I find it excruciating to get the words out.

"It's my friend, Beth, she—she's in trouble. She went to town to see her mother, but her father is a dangerous man; he'll hurt her and—"

"Beth? I don't recall any Beth's at court. What's her family name?"

I pause, at a sudden loss of words. I was hoping to appeal to his sensibilities before he asked that question. I try my best not to cringe as I answer.

"She's not a courtier. She works at the bake house."

For a long, drawn out moment, Father watches me with an unreadable expression. "A servant?" he asks quietly, his head cocked. Then louder, "You are asking me to help a *servant*?"

It's too late to shy from the storm now, might as well dive in. I raise my chin, leveling my eyes to his.

"A *loyal* servant and a dear friend."

Revulsion crosses his face. "Do you expect me to rejoice in this behavior? You suppose I'm proud to know that my own daughter, a *princess*, spends her days with servants?" He pinches the bridge of his nose, lowering his gaze as though he cannot stand the sight of me. "I am glad your mother is not here to live your shame."

I stagger back, recoiling from the invisible knife in my gut.

He directs his chagrin eyes back to me. "If I hear another word of servant friends, I will personally see that they are stripped of their jobs and thrown into the street. Do I make myself clear?"

I feel my fingernails digging into my palms. The helpless anger that heats my skin tells me to stand my ground, to be defiant. But I cannot. If my outburst brought harm to Beth or Holt, or anyone else, I would never forgive myself. I let the thoughts of them cool my temper. I give my father a curt, dark nod.

Satisfied, he takes his leave and barrels out of the room, startling his guards as he shoves past them.

Making sure the way is clear, I rush to the lower east wing of the palace, to Beth's room. If I am to sneak off into town unnoticed, I must do so in disguise. The smell of bread lingers in the air, clinging to her garments and the sheets of her bed. Though it is small, it's much cozier than the vast and empty space of my own chambers. Her bed, unfortunately, is not very comfortable. At least she has a plush, soft pillow I managed to bring for her. I often come to visit Beth after dinner. It is one of the few places where we can relax and just be ourselves, without having to worry about who might be eavesdropping on our conversation. I'm not supposed to come down to this area of the palace, but following rules has never been one of my strong suits.

I rummage through Beth's belongings, looking for something I can wear to disguise myself. Unable to find anything in her drawers, I spot a dirty skirt and bodice. Perfect. The less noticeable I am, the better.

I slip the worn dress on. Beth's garments fit me well enough, though my longer legs make the skirt fall a little short, exposing my ankles and feet. With no cap to wear, I weave my hair into a long braid. It's too bad there is no mirror to look myself over. I'll just have to hope I look the part.

When I cross through the kitchen, I manage to steal a small knife that lies momentarily abandoned on a chopping board full of leafy vegetables. I tell myself it's only a precaution. I can't imagine actually using it. Nevertheless, I feel safer carrying some form of protection.

Today, like any other day, there are plenty of servants running around, and as I had hoped, they are too busy to pay any attention to me. I allow myself to relax a little, loosening up the knot in my chest. With no one in my way, I make a beeline for the back door.

But then, just as I am about to slip through it, someone yells, "Hey Muriel!"

Stomach churning, I pause and quickly glance back. I was hoping there was a Muriel around to respond, but the man's stare is honed in on me. It's one of the cooks, whose name I cannot remember. I keep my head lowered, afraid he will recognize me.

"How many times must I tell you to wear your cap? Are you heading to town with Edsel?"

I stiffen, unsure of how to respond. "Are you just going to stand there like an idiot? Are you or are you not going to town?" he asks, loud and slow.

"Uh, yes," I say, uncertainly.

"Tell him we are also low on salt," he barks, then disappears back into the kitchen.

I sag against the wall. I take a moment to collect myself, and then head out the door before anyone else decides to order me around. I hadn't yet figured out exactly how I would get to town. In my haste to get to Beth, I had not thought that far ahead into my plan. But at this point, hitching a secret ride in the back of a cart with this Edsel person seems like my best option. I comb the area looking for him.

It doesn't take long to find a possible candidate. A young man works on the straps of a horse hitched not to a cart but a covered wagon. *Even better.* Shortly after, he is joined by an older person, and guessing by the feathered hat on his head, he must be the driver. Using the row of large, empty wine barrels for cover, I make my way to the back of the wagon and slowly climb onto it, one hesitant second at a time. The wood squeaks, but the sound is faint under my shoes. Once inside, I curse my luck—it's empty. There is nothing I can use as cover. If anyone happens to peek inside, well, it's not like I can blend with the wood, can I? Not having much choice, I sit and tuck myself into a corner.

To my relief, I hear the men climb onto their seats, the wagon shifting with their weight. The reins snap and off we go. Finally able to relax, I dry my sweaty palms on the flour-and-grease-stained dress. My thoughts shift to Esther and I curl my hands into fists. Of all people, I would have expected her to come through for Beth, no matter what.

With nothing to do but wait, I focus on what I have to do. I don't know where Beth's home is, but the town is small. I should be able to ask around the market square.

If it weren't for the butler, I would have dragged Holt out here with me; Beth couldn't have picked a busier day for him. I'm suddenly angry at her again. She said she did not want my involvement, for obvious reasons. But if I'd known she was planning to go alone, I would have insisted on tagging along. What was she thinking, facing her father all alone? My throat tightens, thinking of the possibility I might be too late. I'm coming, Beth.

The wagon comes to a jolting stop. Conversation, shuffling feet, rolling carts—they all mix and mingle into a distinctive roar. A drastic change from the quiet palace. I remember feeling overwhelmed the first time I was here.

I wait until Edsel leaves for the shops before I climb out of the wagon, making sure the driver does not notice me. The mud-caked square is filled with shop boards where merchants and traders display their wares. The town of Windermere is one of the many merchant towns of Stonefall, and the closest to the palace. Consequently, it's the only one I've visited. People come and go, baskets in hand, buying and trading with tailors, glovers, and butchers. Wooden shop signs on metal hooks display the names and insignias of each shop, though they typically never correlate to the product on display. Take the fishmonger's shop, for example, with a carved pot on his sign, the words *The Lucky Cauldron* engraved above it. The briny scent of the fish on his board travels freely across the square, assaulting my nose, masking all other smells. I can't even get a whiff of the raw meat under attack by the butcher's cleaver, whose shop, *The Green Dragon*, lies only a few feet away. Across the square, a small crowd gathers around the town crier, but there is too much noise around me to hear. Beyond and around the square are the tenements, timber-framed homes of thatched roofs and willowy plaster. They crowd together, narrow and tall; most are two or three stories, with timber jetties projecting out of each level.

I hone in on the flower girl who strolls around at her leisure, weaving in and out of people's way, oblivious to impatience.

I ask after Beth's family name, and the little girl's eyes light up with interest. "The drunkard's home?"

I nod enthusiastically. "Yes."

"My mum told me to stay away from his house," she says, biting her lower lip.

"You don't have to take me there, just tell me where to go."

She gives me a dubious look, clearly wondering why I want to go into the lion's den. In the end, she just shrugs. With simple directions, she instructs which streets to take, telling me to look for the "ugly" cottage in Riverside Street.

"You won't miss it," she says with a giggle.

She's right. You would have to be blind not to notice it. The single-story house is clearly neglected, its wood rotted, giving the impression it will collapse any day. Its thatched roof, with gaping holes and frayed edges, looks tenuous. Even in broad daylight, the house seems eerie. I take a turn around the house, hoping to find an open window to peek through. To my dismay, all the shutters are tightly sealed. The thought that perhaps Beth has come and gone crosses my mind for a fleeting second. If she has, I will find out soon enough. I approach the front door cautiously and listen. The weakness in my legs urges me to turn around and run as fast as I can. But I can't think about what I am doing. I've come all this way, I can't turn back now. I clutch at the small knife in my hand, hoping to still my nerves.

I press my ear against the door. Silence. I knock. Once. Twice. No one comes. I try the knob, expecting it to be locked. It turns freely in my hand. I let out a low breath and steel myself for whatever awaits me. I grit my teeth at the squeal of the door when I push it open.

Inside, the air is stale, permeated with the bitter stench of ale. Leaving the door wide open behind me, I glance around nervously, taking in the eerie emptiness of the place. Its silence screams loudly at me. It's a small house, so small that it's a little suffocating. I expected to find the signs of a violent aftermath. Yet all I see before me are a chair and a small table, undisturbed and set neatly in place. A light shines on them from one of the holes in the roof. Dust particles glint under the light, telling a tale of disuse. A cobwebbed stove is unlit and forgotten.

"Beth?" I whisper in a shaky voice. I pause to listen, but all I hear are the cautious creaks and groans of my steps on the floorboards.

I shift to the tips of my toes and walk in the direction of the only other room in the house, its door slightly ajar. Peering inside, my eyes widen as they find a woman, presumably Beth's mother. She lies in bed like a corpse, still as a stone. Her arms are stretched out at her sides. *Is she...?* I swallow hard and approach the foot of the bed. That's when I notice a figure crumpled on the floor at the other side of the bed.

Heart thumping, I hold my breath and lean forward. It only takes me a moment to register the familiar chocolate shade of her hair.

"Beth!"

In a panic, I scramble to her side. Her childlike face is marred by swollen skin and open gashes. I grab her by the shoulders and shake her limp body. "Beth!"

Hot tears prick my eyes. "Beth, please wake up," I say weakly, my voice threatening to crack.

Just as I recognize the sound of approaching steps, hands latch onto my arms, yanking me to my feet, and I am flying, crashing against the wall.

A bald, bearded man wearing a heavily soiled shirt and torn trousers glares at me. Beth's father. The reek of ale is pungent and bitter, burning my nose as though I am smelling it straight from a bottle. My knife is across the floor, out of reach. I must have dropped it when he tossed me aside.

Beth's father seems to notice this. Still glaring, he kicks it away with a flick of his foot.

"What are you doing in my house?" he asks. His words slur and yet they sound calculated and menacing.

I stand on shaky legs. "I am here for Beth," I say, as defiant as a mouse to a cat.

His eyes narrow into slits. "She's not going anywhere." *And neither are you*, his eyes seem to say.

He is ready to charge me, and I have nothing but my empty hands to defend myself with. The only thing to do is run, but I cannot abandon Beth. I can't leave her to her father's mercy. But I can't fight him either. So I use the only leverage I have.

"I am Princess Meredith, and I am here to bring Beth back to the palace," I try to demand, but my voice betrays me.

"You lying wench. You take me for a fool?"

Then, in the fraction of a moment, his fist connects with my cheek, so hard I lose my balance. For a moment, my vision is cloudy with dancing circles of lights. Then, as my vision clears, I feel the stinging, throbbing pain of the blow.

"You think you can just trespass into my home and take my family away? They are mine," he says, leering.

He reaches for me and pulls me back up, slamming my back against the wall, pushing the air out of my lungs.

The man's eyes twist with a crazed rage. He brings his hands around my neck and squeezes. I clutch at them, digging my nails into his skin, but this only seems to fuel his madness. He squeezes harder, burning my skin with the friction of his force. The room around me begins to dim, shadows creeping at the edges of my vision. If I don't do something now, I won't have the strength to do anything else, and he will kill me. Panic takes over. I thrash my legs wildly with a burst of manic energy. Inadvertently, this makes him take a step back, giving me enough room to hike a knee into his groin. He releases me and I drop to my hands and knees. I cough and start to crawl away, slowly regaining the strength in my legs until I'm able to stand up and run.

I am halfway out the front door when he catches me by the back of my dress and shoves me back inside. I scream but my throat is so hoarse it is almost inaudible.

"Stupid girl," he sneers.

I am stupid, for thinking I could defend myself. If he hadn't caught me off guard, if I hadn't lost hold of the knife, then I might have stood a chance. But I'm not dead yet. And as long as I'm still alive, I have a chance.

The man approaches me, towering above me, raising his arm like an executioner about to deal a deadly blow. But as it comes down at me, I whirl out of the way. I dart back into the bedroom, my eyes on the knife. But just as my fingers graze the hilt, I feel something under my legs. I fall flat on my face, ignore the pain, and reach for the knife. As I grab hold of the handle, he brings his foot down on it, stomping my hand. I cry out. He kicks me over to my back so I can see him. He smiles a joyless smile.

I tense, bringing my arms and legs up defensively, and shut my eyes. A loud thump follows, shaking the floor around me. Cautiously, I lower my arms.

Beth's father lies unconscious on the floor. Next to him stands an alluring stranger, who, from the straps that cross his torso, appears to be fully armed, though he holds no weapons in his hands. A pair of dark leather arm guards cover the sleeves of his shirt at his wrists. He kneels, leveling a serious gaze at me. Tousled black hair frames the handsome face. A long, pale scar runs from his left brow down to his cheek, creating a small gap in the shape of his brow.

"Are you wounded?" he asks in a deep, steady voice.

I gape at him, bewildered. I would answer, only my head is too preoccupied trying to comprehend what just happened.

"I...who are you?" I croak.

He frowns at me with what appears to be annoyance. Swiftly, he stands and pulls me to my feet. I'm not sure if I should thank him or snap at him, but before I can say anything he is walking around me, giving me the once-over. I try unsuccessfully to find a place for my suddenly awkward hands.

His deep-set eyes are dark, shrouded, and all together severe. And yet there is something about them, something about the way he looks through them that piques my interest.

"Are you the princess?" he asks me.

I narrow my eyes. "Who sent you?"

He quirks his eyebrows. "So it's you then. Good. And your friend, is she all right?" he asks, raising his chin at Beth's body.

I kneel by her side. Her skin feels cold to the touch. As I examine her wounded face, a dull heaviness creeps into my chest. Beth needed me. She needed my help. And I failed her.

The stranger walks to the bed and presses two fingers against Beth's mother's neck.

"Dead," I hear him whisper.

He looks over at me, then at Beth, then back at me. For a moment, he stares as though he is studying me, as though I am some strange creature he cannot figure out.

"Is your friend alive?" he asks.

"Yes," I blurt out, as if saying it out loud will make it true. She can't be dead. Slowly, I place my hand just below her nose.

My stomach knots with anticipation. *Please, please, please.* It seems like an eternity before I register the subtle breath coming from her nostrils.

A shaky laugh bubbles out of me. She's alive.

"Will you help me?" I ask the stranger.

He nods and reaches for Beth. He picks her up like she doesn't weigh a thing, nestling her body between his arms.

"Let's go," he says, and I follow him outside.

Walking behind him, I get a full view of the bow and quiver strapped to his broad-shouldered back. As far as I can tell, this man, whoever he is, must be well trained in combat. Could this be the escort Father spoke of this morning? I can't be sure. He did just save my life though—and Beth's. Could he be a spy? The thought makes me stop half-stride. Is he an assassin? One of King Theros' men?

Keep it together, Meredith. Now is not the time to panic. Not while he has Beth in his arms. Whoever this handsome, well-armed stranger is, he seems to know a lot about me.

A black saddled horse waits outside, the reins tied around a post. The animal is a beast, larger than any horse I've ever ridden on.

"Will you be able to hold her on the horse?" the stranger asks, gesturing down at Beth, who dangles limply in his arms.

"Yes," I answer, grateful for the tedious riding lessons I was forced to attend growing up.

I latch on to the stirrup and push up onto the saddle. He hands Beth up to me and I help him, pulling her up from underneath her arms. I struggle with her weight, but he lifts her high enough to where I can manage to sit her on the saddle. As I settle Beth in, her body sags onto me. I am about to fall sideways when a hand catches my back and pushes me forward.

"Thank you," I say as our eyes lock. Ignoring the traitorous flush of heat that sneaks into my cheeks, I wrap my arms around Beth and ask, "What about you?"

"I'll walk," he says evenly.

Though the palace is not far, it's not close enough to travel by foot, at least not comfortably. But I suppose for a man like him, it must not be that taxing.

"You never gave me your name," I say.

"You never asked for it," he answers.

It takes me a moment to process that he deliberately thwarted my question. I frown. "Yes I did. I asked you."

"You didn't ask for my name. There's a difference." I find his nonchalance irritating.

"No there isn't," I scoff. "Wanting to know who you are implies that I want to know your name."

He ignores me and walks ahead.

If only he'd turn around and look at me. I want to throw my shoe at him, but then I remind myself that he is helping me. He's helping Beth. I swallow heavily. "All right," I say slowly. "What is your name then?"

"Connor."

Now we are getting somewhere. "And who sent you looking for me?" I ask, a little apprehensive at the thought that I might not like what he has to say.

"I volunteered."

"Volunteered?" I ask, perplexed. When had my little outing been discovered? "I'm not sure I follow."

"I met your chambermaid on her way to ask the king to send the entire royal guard after you, when she learned where you had gone. I thought it unnecessary, so I volunteered."

So he came from the palace. Could this be my escort? But he does own a horse, and the long, soft leather boots and black jerkin he wears atop a white linen shirt indicate he is of a certain status. Gentry at the very least; not common attire for a soldier.

"What's your title?"

"I don't have a title. I'm a soldier."

A wealthy soldier, it seems. An inheritance, perhaps? "I guess soldiers for hire get far better wages than the poor fellows under my father's rule," I prod.

This time he turns to look at me, his gaze lingering, a flicker of curiosity flashing in those intense eyes of his. I fight the urge to look away.

"I'm a soldier of Alder. Your escort," he says finally.

I am both relieved and annoyed. Relieved that he is not some deranged killer out to dismember me. Annoyed that I will be forced to spend months with such a frustrating, tight-lipped, unnervingly reserved man.

But then his words sink in. "Wait, you've come from Alder? Why would my father send for one of you?"

"It was my king who sent me here, not yours," he says.

Sent by King Perceval? His answers only seem to leave me with more questions. "Why? I thought the alliance was on delicate grounds."

"Solidarity?" he muses with a shrug, not at all concerned. It shouldn't surprise me, his kingdom isn't on the chopping block. To him, this is just another job.

"Does my father know?" I ask Anabella when we're back at the palace. She shakes her head. We sit on a pair of chairs in my rooms. She dips a face cloth into a bowl of cold water and dabs it on the swollen green and purple bruise on my cheekbone.

Upon arriving at the palace, I found her in a state of distress, pacing about the front gate with her palm fast to her heart. She was overjoyed when I returned, but now she is all too keen on reprimanding me. She presses the wet cloth against my cheek.

"That hurts!" I complain, pushing her hand away.

"Do you have any idea what a fright you gave me?"

I know very well, though that won't stop her from scolding me every five minutes until she feels she has punished me enough.

"I'm sorry," I say. "I was only trying to help."

At this, her eyes soften a little. "Yes child, I know," she says, lightly patting my hand. "But you cannot behave so brashly, not with a target on that pretty little head of yours."

"I don't have a death wish, Anabella. It's just...if I hadn't gone, Beth—"

"She would be dead," Anabella finishes for me. "And if Sir Westwend had not gone after you, *you* would be dead as well," she says, prodding an accusatory finger into my chest.

"Connor?"

"Your escort," Anabella nods.

I groan. "That man is insufferable."

"He's not here to earn your good graces, dear."

"He's not here to irritate me either," I point out. "It doesn't matter. Is there any word from the physician yet?"

"I'm sure he is still tending to Beth."

"I'll go see her then," I say, standing up.

Anabella lays a hand on my wrist. "Don't fret, child. You have done enough for today. Let her rest. You can see her in the morning."

I slump back into my chair, sulking. I am eager to find out if Beth is awake. But having spent the entire afternoon playing heroics, I suppose it's a little late to be wandering about the palace.

Anabella drops the cloth in the bowl. "That's about all I can do. You'd better have a good story for your father tomorrow."

I pick up the hand mirror, gripping its gold handle. The bruise does not look any better than it did a few minutes ago, but the swelling has gone down considerably. "I could always keep to my rooms. There are plenty of books I've yet to read."

"That would be an excellent idea...if you didn't have rehearsal tomorrow," she reminds me, picking up the bowl and sauntering to the bathing room.

The rehearsal.

I really am terrible at remembering appointments. It's the first waltz rehearsal for the annual ball, which requires all unmarried ladies of court to attend, myself included. It's a shame being engaged doesn't exempt me, which means I will have to show up, bruised face and all, and struggle like I always do to move my two left feet to Lady Amelia's impossible choreography.

Charlotte is going to love this, I think to myself, staring at the violet contusion on my face.

Chapter Four

When I first step into the courtyard, the ladies are busy talking among themselves. To my relief, no one pays me any attention, save for a sideways glance. It's not long, however, before someone spots my bruise and gasps, which instantly silences all conversation. They whisper and murmur to each other. I spot Charlotte, her lips curling in amusement. *So predictable.* She turns and whispers something to her best friend, Geneve. They both look up at me and giggle.

Lady Amelia steps forth from behind the group of girls and curtsies. "Your *highness*." Her steely gray eyes thoroughly scrutinize me. She raises an index finger to her cheek and gives me a slight shake of the head.

I bite my lower lip. Though I don't necessarily like Lady Amelia, I have always regarded her with some degree of respect. She carries herself with such delicate grace and refinement that you can only hope to be like her. And despite her age, she maintains a youthful appearance. I know that I will only disappoint her; I am far too clumsy to ever earn her much sought-after approval.

"Is everything all right?" she asks softly, gingerly clasping her hands together.

"Yes," I say quickly. "It was just a little accident. Nothing to be concerned about." I flash the most apologetic smile I can muster.

"Well," she says dismissively and twirls around to face the rest of the girls. "Now that we are all here, let's begin, shall we?"

Lady Amelia orders us into place. I can sense her distaste as she instructs me to the center of the line. I am not any happier than she is at being the focus of the waltz. No matter how much I concentrate, how much I dedicate myself to practicing the steps, or how much help I get from Beth and Anabella, when the time comes to perform, I never fail to stand out like a twig amid a bed of flowers.

Charlotte, who just so happens to be Lady Amelia's favorite, is ordered to stand next to me in the formation.

"You should lay off catching rabbits with your teeth, cousin, it does not bode well for your face," she whispers sweetly.

I grit my teeth. "How instructive you are, cousin."

"It's the least I can do." I don't have to look at her to see the venomous smile plastered on her face.

Lady Amelia calls for our silence and attention. She begins by explaining the changes and additions to last year's waltz. Swift, prancing steps become a jumbled mess in my head, and beads of sweat suddenly sprout on my forehead. For every two steps I take, I find myself making a mistake. At this rate, I'll take a tumble before our first break.

When the time comes to hold hands, I grudgingly reach for Charlotte. She smiles innocently as she squeezes my hand, so tightly it begins to feel numb.

Two can play that game.

I curl my fingers around her hand, digging my nails into her skin. I hear Charlotte hiss under her breath and she relaxes her hold.

Lady Amelia instructs us, one step at a time, watching us repeat the moves until they become second nature. I doubt my execution is anywhere close to my peers', but I manage to follow without tripping over my own feet until Lady Amelia calls for a rest.

Then, as if on cue, servants ceremoniously come to provide us with refreshments. I am relieved to see a familiar face among them. Holt discreetly taps a finger to his cheekbone and gives me an approving thumbs up, his mouth teasing at the corner. *I'm glad my bruise amuses you*, I think, scowling in his direction. A long table is set. Atop it, servants place several silver platters of food and gold-trimmed cups. As is custom, a cup made of pure gold is brought for me. Holt and another boy fill them to the brim with wine.

The ladies flock to the table and quickly resume their gossip, sipping wine and stuffing pastries into their mouths.

I ogle the glasses of wine. I could probably drink several of them. One will have to do. I make my way to the table, but as I approach, Geneve deliberately picks up my gold cup and, glancing back at me, she takes a sip out of it. I chuckle. They can drink out of that silly gold cup all they want for all I care. I pick up one of the generic cups. They are watching me, of course, so I raise my cup to them and wink. They glare back at me with disdain.

I inch my way to one of the trimmed bushes, far enough away where I don't have to listen to the latest fashion trends of foreign kingdoms. I pretend to be fascinated by the shiny foliage and bring the cup of wine to my lips. But as I do, a blood-curdling shriek fills the air. I whirl around. Before I can pinpoint the source, the girls crumble into a chorus of screams and hysterics. Cups smash to the ground.

The group frantically backs away from Geneve. Blood pours from her mouth and nose as she heaves and chokes, her hands clutching at her throat. A horrified Charlotte screams beside her.

I watch, rooted in place, as the scene unfolds before my eyes. I am confused, not entirely sure of what is happening, of what I'm witnessing. In a matter of seconds, Geneve lies dead on the ground.

An eerie sensation sinks into me, and I want to blink it away, to pinch myself, to join in with screams of my own. I want to wake up.

I cannot peel my eyes away from Geneve's body, but then someone steps in and blocks my view. I feel something slap at my hand and I lose my grip on the cup of wine I'd forgotten I was holding. It falls to the grass with a muffled thump. A pair of hands shake me by the shoulders. I register Connor's face.

"Did you drink the wine?" he asks hurriedly.

My gaze darts past him back to Geneve, then to the gold cup next to her, the wine spilled on the ground.

Poison. The wine was poisoned. No one else appears to have been affected. Only my cup. Someone tried to kill me. Had it not been for Geneve and Charlotte's taunting, it would be me dead on the ground. The realization squeezes the air out of my lungs and a queasy feeling overturns my stomach. The palace has always been safe, a respite from the troubles of the outside world.

And now, that sense of security ebbs away, as if the palace walls are crumbling. I feel exposed to King Theros, to all his lackeys, like I am up for the taking.

Connor shakes me again. "Princess."

He is looking at me, his eyes stern, urgent. He stands so close that I notice they are not black, as I had originally thought, but a dark blue.

I shake my head slowly.

"Do you remember which servant filled your cup?"

The images in my head flash out of sequence, an inconsistent recollection of Holt and the other boy filling the cups; I hadn't paid enough attention. But it doesn't matter, I already know the answer.

"It wasn't him," I mutter.

At that moment, guards storm the courtyard. The screaming has stopped, replaced by sobs and whimpers. Some of the girls have found comfort with one another, huddled together, holding on to each other's arms and hands.

One of the guards takes Geneve in his arms and rushes her away. Charlotte glares at me through tears. And then, with determined strides, she charges toward me.

To my surprise and immense relief, Connor blocks her way, using his body as a barricade.

"You killed her! You killed Geneve!" she yells at me, thrashing violently against Connor's restraint. Charlotte tries to get around him, screaming, but he grips her by the arms, holding her in place. It's strange to see her so out of control. It's the first time I feel afraid of her.

When she doesn't relent, Connor hands her over to one of the guards, saying something in his ear. The guard hauls her back inside the palace.

In spite of myself, I can't help but feel sorry for her. Geneve was her best friend. Yesterday, I almost lost mine. I can easily admit that I dislike Charlotte, and yet I would never wish her this suffering. I will not overlook her faults and the things she has said and done against me. But I cannot hold this against her.

I am pulled out of my thoughts by a commotion. Guards tow two young men past, their unwilling feet dragging and scraping against the hard, white stone of the courtyard walkway.

Holt.

"It was them!" says one of the ladies.

"Yes," adds Lady Amelia, who for once does not look so composed, her hair slightly out of place, her arms fidgety.

"No, please!" pleads the boy, whose name I do not know. "Someone else filled her cup—we didn't know it was poisoned, I swear it!"

A guard slams a fist in his face. "Silence!"

I cannot know if the boy is telling the truth in regards to his own involvement, but I am not about to let that doubt drag Holt along with him to the scaffold.

"Release those boys at once!" I demand of the guards.

For a moment, everyone looks confused. More than a dozen pair of eyes bulge.

"Your highness," says one of the guards. "These servants have committed treason."

"You have no proof. They served the wine, that much is true, but it does not mean they are the ones who poisoned it," I reply, my voice stern and unwavering.

"But your highness, it is procedure—"

"I *said* release them."

Though they hesitate at first, the guards consent, releasing the wine bearers. The boy rushes to express his gratitude. He kneels before me.

"Maker bless you for your mercy, your highness," he says.

I motion for him to stand. "Please, that's not necessary. What is your name?"

"James Cromwell, your highness," he stammers.

"Meredith, that cup was already filled," Holt mutters under his breath, his face pale. "We were supposed to serve the wine out here, with all the rest. I didn't think anything of it—I should have said something."

"And you are sure it wasn't him?" I ask, nodding at James,

who whimpers at my question.

Holt pats James gently on the back. "We were together the entire time, your highness."

"Come with me," Connor says suddenly, his eyes locked on James and Holt.

I spin my head in his direction. "What do you want with them?"

"I have questions," he explains, though he says this more to them than to me, as he doesn't look my way once. Holt glances at me questioningly. I return an encouraging nod and Connor ushers them away. I may not care much for him, but I can't deny the comforting feeling in my core that tells me I can trust him.

Chapter Five

Beth does not look good, her face and arms swollen with dark bruises. At least she claims to feel much better. Inside her crowded room, the penetrating scent of herbal ointments makes my head ache, a faint throb emerging in between my brows. I glance at the culprits, spread out on her nightstand. The mortar and pestle is halfway full with some waxy-looking substance, drops of oil splashed on three glass containers filled with yellow and brown liquids.

When Beth mentions Esther spent the night watching over her, I bite back a sarcastic comment. I want to tell her about Esther, but I know that knowledge will only hurt her, so I decide to keep it to myself. Instead, I tell her what happened to Geneve.

Rattled, she sits upright on her small bed. "Is Holt all right?"

"Yes," I assure her, trying not to sound as paranoid as I feel. I hate that Holt has been forced into such dangerous ground. I can only hope that he will have the answers to finding the one responsible. My hair stands on end, thinking of what Father might do if he doesn't believe in Holt's innocence.

"What happens now?" Beth asks.

"I don't know," I shrug. "Tighten security, maybe?"

"Good thing your escort is here."

I make a face at her. "Wait until you get to know him."

"He's handsome," she adds with a smile.

"You've met him?" I ask, surprised.

"Yes, he was here."

"Here?" I ask.

She nods. "Early this morning. He wanted to make sure I was all right."

I sit up straighter. "That's odd."

"He's not a man of many words, is he?" she asks.

We stare at each other for a brief second before we both snort and break down into silly giggles, Beth half-laughing, half-grimacing from the pain.

When we quiet down, Beth is more serious. "He saved our lives, Mer."

I let out a slow breath as I nod in agreement. If Connor had not come for me, we'd both be dead by now.

"I cannot believe you went looking for me," she mutters.

Then I remember why I was mad at her. "And I cannot believe you lied to me about going home. Why did you not tell me?"

"Because it was dangerous," she explains as though I don't already know this. "I can afford to risk my life. But you?"

"That doesn't mean you should."

"I had no choice, Mer."

The memory of her mother's corpse on the bed flashes in my mind. "Did you get a chance to say good-bye?" I ask softly.

She looks away. "No," she whispers. "She was already gone when I arrived."

I hate to see her like this, wounded inside and out. And I hate not being able to do anything about it.

"I'm so glad I didn't lose you too. I love you, Mer," she says, tears spilling down her cheeks.

It had been foolish and risky to go after Beth like that. But if I hadn't, no one would have come for her. I would have lost her.

I wrap my arms around her. "I love you too."

People at court don't take the news of Geneve's death too well. In the two days that have passed, fear has settled in as the new resident of the palace. You can see the paranoia in people's darting eyes and pale faces. They go about their day in murmurs and whispers. The grim ambiance of the palace only serves to heighten the dreary sense of unpredictable doom. If only I knew who poisoned the wine, I could sleep a little easier at night. If Connor has learned anything, he has yet to mention it to me. I would ask him about it, except I have not seen him at all since the day of the rehearsal. With everything that's going on, I would have expected him to be around more. I can only assume he's investigating.

Oppressed by the walls in my room, I find much-needed fresh air in the outer courtyard. Rays of light pour down through the broken, scattered pattern of the canopy. I soak in the sun, letting it warm my chilled cheeks. The air is crisp and enlivening. I close my eyes and breathe. I needed this, needed to be alone, removed from my own thoughts and away from everyone else's.

The waltz has been canceled and the tournament postponed for a few days, out of respect for Geneve's family. I suppose that is the only good thing to come out of it, although my relief comes laced with the heavy weight of a guilty conscience. It's been a struggle to adjust to the abrupt changes. When Father learned of the incident, he enlisted tasters to inspect all food and drink before it's served to me. But after the first few meals, I could not take it anymore. The anxiety of anticipating the tasters to start oozing blood and convulsing before my eyes was too much to handle, so I asked Anabella to witness them in my stead.

I feel incredible guilt over Geneve's death. It's not that I believe it to be my fault that she died, as Charlotte so eloquently pointed out, but I cannot help feeling somewhat responsible. The poison had been meant for me. Geneve saved my life. The worst of it is the relief I feel. Relief that it was her and not me, not because she deserved it, because no one deserves to die so young and in such a horrible way, but because of the fear that shakes me when I recall the blood oozing out of her mouth, choking her.

"What's the matter?"

Charles, having appeared suddenly, peers at me, concern glazing his eyes.

I've been so wrapped up in my thoughts that I did not even notice my hand clutching my throat.

"You're a sight for sore eyes, cousin," I say, ignoring propriety and hugging him.

"Sore eyes indeed," he jests with a chuckle, pointing at my face.

"I thought a black eye would look rather nice. Don't you? All the courtiers are raving about it."

Charles throws his head back, laughing. "And I thought it was just another featherbrained fabrication the ladies concocted. But I stand corrected. You are a true trendsetter, dear cousin. How did you manage to acquire such a fashionable accessory?"

"It's a long story," I sigh. "And not a very pleasant one, either."

He lets out a low whistle, hooking my arm around his. "Long, unpleasant stories. My favorite."

We walk along the narrow trail that circles the courtyard while I recount the events that led to the unsightly bruise on my face, starting from the moment I left his company the day of the tournament to when I arrived back in the palace. The gravel crunches beneath our feet. A cool breeze sweeps gently against us as we stroll on. Charles listens in reserved silence, his eyes fixed ahead on the trail.

He remains quiet when I finish, his face blank, void of any expression to hint at his thoughts. I struggle with the idea that perhaps he, for the very first time, might disapprove of my actions, and a sliver of worry shoots through my chest. I can handle disappointing everyone, even Father, but not Charles.

Brimming with anxiety, I'm about to say something when he turns sideways to look at me. His lips break into a soft smile. "You will make a great queen one day."

I let out a shaky laugh.

"Don't be silly. You and I both know queens are only the king's shadow. You, on the other hand, would be the best king the world has ever known. It's a shame you are not next in line to the throne. If it were up to me, I'd gladly hand it over to you."

"Don't let my father hear you say that," he says with a snort.

He jokes, though we both know how right he is. The duke is a greedy man and has made it very clear it is his wish for Charles to be the heir to the throne. His efforts have paid off in securing Charles' place as the crown prince in the event anything happened to me prior to marriage.

As we continue our walk, I sense a change in Charles' demeanor when his arm tenses under my hand. "Cousin, I never thought I'd say this, but I cannot wait for you to marry the prince," he says.

Coming from him, it's a very strange thing to say.

"You don't mean that," I say after a short, awkward silence.

He sighs. "I do. I'll miss you terribly, but it is not safe for you here. Not anymore. I have this dreadful feeling that things will get much, much worse." The stress in his voice is jarringly bizarre. Charles, who all his life has been happy and content, seems like a stranger, stiff with worry and unease.

"My escort will protect me," I say, wanting to find a reason not to agree with him. Because I do agree. I want to be safe and not have to worry about my food and drink or watching my back at every corner. It's been only two days and I'm already exhausted. How will I manage month after month of this? But safety does not guarantee happiness, and I highly doubt I'll be happy in the life of servitude imposed by marriage.

"Of course he will. But he is just one man. And where is he now? You were out here all alone when I found you."

"She wasn't alone," comes a voice from behind.

Startled, we whip around, our eyes searching the bushes. Charles steps in front of me, cautioning me to stay back.

My breath quickens. Someone *had* been watching us. Movement above catches my eye. Connor crouches in a tree off to my right, feet firmly rooted to a thick branch, his hand casually resting against the trunk as though climbing up trees is a common, leisure activity.

"It's all right, Charles, it's just my escort," I say, keeping my eyes locked on Connor.

I walk up to the foot of the tree. "What are you doing up there?" I ask, as Charles comes up beside me.

"Watching you."

"You followed me?" I raise an accusatory brow at him. "Why?"

"Because you make poor decisions," he says.

I clench my fists at my sides.

Connor makes his way down, gliding through the branches. He jumps down from the lowest branch, landing on his feet with his knees slightly bent. He straightens and takes a few steps toward me, coming uncomfortably close. Once more, I find myself under the intensity of his bewildering gaze, and my fingers begin to twitch.

"Why do you not do as you are told?" he asks, his voice low and controlled.

My mouth drops, taken aback. Just who does he think he is? Why does he feel as though I owe him an explanation? His job is to protect me, not to question me.

I take a step closer, refusing to be intimidated. He is tall enough that I have to tilt my head up to face him. "That is none of your concern," I say, pleased at how calm I sound, despite my ruffled feathers.

We stand so close our noses almost brush together. Unlike me, however, the closeness does not appear to faze him.

"If you insist on wandering off on your own, you give me no choice but to follow." He speaks in a casual, straightforward manner that clashes with the standoffish coldness in his eyes.

Must I be robbed of every freedom in the name of safety? I want to say that I am aware of the danger, that I glance over my shoulder every time I think about it. That I am afraid for my life. What I cannot say is why, in spite of it all, my feet seem to have walked outside of their own accord and didn't think twice about it.

"Sir, I believe you have irritated my cousin quite enough," Charles interjects, gesturing with an outstretched hand for me to join him. *Indeed he has.*

I'm turning to leave when Connor catches my arm by the crook of the elbow. "The wine was poisoned with Nightlok," he whispers in my ear.

Nightlok. Small bright-red berries, so toxic they cause severe skin reactions with a mere touch. My mind flashes to tales of murder and intrigue I've paged through in the palace library. The seed is very rare. It doesn't even grow in Stonefall, and possession of it is illegal. It can only be purchased through the bootleg market at a very high price. Whoever is involved, it's someone well endowed.

"I would advise you keep in your cousin's company," Connor tells me before I walk away.

Which I do. I hook my arm around Charles, where it remains for the rest of the day.

The next morning, a crowd of sullen faces forms the funeral procession. Above us, the skies are painted a dull gray, covered in a uniform blanket of clouds. The church bells are somber. Some walk in quiet misery, others voice their anguish with broken sobs, while a few weep and cry. I want to tell them I'm sorry for their loss. I want to say nice things about Geneve, even though I don't have anything nice to say. Instead, I keep my head down and focus on placing one steady foot before the other. I walk closely behind my father, who leads the lazy river of black-clad people to the palace graveyard. A few steps behind us, servants carry a coffin draped in black, surrounded by Geneve's parents, her brother and three younger sisters. Geneve's mother and sisters wear black veils that provide a sense of privacy to their grief, hiding their mourning faces from the rest of us.

Connor walks beside me, clad in a white shirt and double-breasted black vest with a tall collar. He'd been waiting for me outside my rooms this morning. I was briefly distracted by how unexpectedly dashing he looked, and found myself struggling to speak coherently. But I was saved by his impatience as he quickly explained, with as few words as possible, that he was to remain at my side through the duration of the funeral. As the entire court would be present, the murderer might be among them. So I was more than happy to oblige.

A gaping hole awaits us at the graveyard. Rows upon rows of headstones line the grassy field. Many are so old and covered in moss that you can no longer read the name of the person buried beneath them. They lie there, reminding us of our mortality in a stark silence of death. Even the grass, green and thick and full of life, is disfigured by the peppered bald spots and well-worn trails that expose the soil. Slowly, we assemble around the empty grave and watch as Geneve's coffin is lowered into the ground.

Dressed in a golden robe, a priest of the Order steps forth, the book of the Maker in hand, to orate a eulogy. He reads the traditional passage of life and death, and speaks of how Geneve is now one with the Maker, but as I lift my head up I catch a glimpse of Charlotte, and I stop listening. She stands on the opposite side of the grave, arms stiffly pressed against her sides, her mouth set into a white, thin line, and her eyes dark, burning with a wrath I feel ignite under my skin, spreading into a scorching fire. I thought these last few days would have served to clear her mind and soften her resentment; I guess it's too soon for that. She glares as if it were me who poisoned the wine. Neither of us looks away.

The priest finishes his speech, and after a short pause, my father speaks. As king, it is his duty to bring honor to Geneve's family in the wake of their loss. I have attended enough funerals that I can almost recite his tributes, which merely rehash what he's said scores of times before. There are never any personal anecdotes, nothing to speak of the deceased as an individual. But then, as my glaring contest with Charlotte continues, I hear something that snaps me back into focus.

"...they work for the enemy and are therefore our enemies. They will not go unpunished. They will pay for their treason. Tomorrow at this hour, we will have justice."

I stare at the crowd of mourners. Conviction brightens their doleful eyes. When was the culprit found?

I open my mouth to ask Connor about it but I stop, noticing

he is fixed on Father, who dismisses everyone, announcing the funeral is over. The court disperses, taking their leave in clusters as if they've just watched a jousting match come to an end. I watch for Charlotte, half-expecting her to come at me again with all her fury, but there is no sign of her. Then, as people clear from around the open grave, servants come up to it. They drag a cart full of dirt behind them, shovels in hand. It strikes me as odd that they all look unusually pale, their skin pasty white, their gaze distant.

Father takes his leave, advisers and guards parading after him. Connor's gaze follows him. Even after he has stepped out of sight, Connor does not look away.

It's not long before only Connor and I remain with the servants, who shovel dirt in Geneve's grave.

"What is it?" I ask.

Anger rims his eyes. "He knows they're innocent," he mutters.

"Who's innocent?"

"James and Holt," he says.

"Of course they are," I agree. And then understanding hits me like a sack of potatoes.

"*That's* who my father just sentenced to death?" I ask in a suddenly high-pitched voice.

Connor gives me a sharp nod. I picture Holt, hands bound,

dragged up the stairs of the scaffold, where a hooded headsman waits for him, axe in hand. A disturbing fear courses through my veins. They are to be punished for a crime they never committed, which is what the murderer intended all along. It's wrong. It's all wrong. The sickness I feel is reflected in Connor's eyes, in the pale faces of the servants shoveling dirt.

"But the Nightlok...? Can't you speak with my father about it?"

"I already have. Servants don't have the means to purchase the seeds, and he knows it. It's possible that members of the staff are involved, through bribery or threats, but the mole is someone of wealth and resources," he says.

"He is attempting to appease the court, to hand them someone to blame, a scapegoat," I say with a hiss, thinking of Charlotte.

"And to squash rumors of an enemy among us. He is doing this to maintain control," he adds.

Fear strikes me cold, sinking its teeth into my flesh. Holt is innocent. And so is James. They can't be executed. The wheels in my head spin. I won't let it happen. I *can't* let it happen. But I don't have much time.

Chapter Six

Hours later, I hurry through the courtyard as the sun sets over the horizon, its warm, deep orange and yellow rays are singed with streaks of pink. Soon the temperature will drop, bringing the chill of the night. It wasn't easy to rid myself of Connor. I practically had to lock myself in my rooms, feigning a very bad headache. I half-expected him to be outside my door waiting for me when I popped out, but there were only the guards on watch. Thankfully, those two have no desire to follow me around. I suppose Connor really did believe I would rest and take supper in my rooms.

Shortly after the funeral, Father left the palace to go duck hunting. I took advantage of his absence to sneak into his study and stamp a letter with his official seal. I knew this was the only way the guards would grant James and Holt exit from the palace gates without asking questions. The door ward didn't question me when I walked in under the pretense of leaving a note for my father, and I made sure to hide the letter inside my bodice before I left. I realize this will cost me my liberties; Father will make sure I am not allowed anywhere without supervision. Scurrying along, I lift the heavy, embroidered fabric of my dress to keep from tripping on it. I had hoped to make it to the jail earlier, but preparing a bag of provisions and saddling the horse took longer than I had anticipated. Now I can only pray that the jailers won't get suspicious. Beth, horrified as she was, had insisted on helping, but I refused. I could not involve her in this. I could not risk her being caught and punished. Punishment enough awaits me. I can already see the anger in my father's eyes, hear the rage in his voice. But that's not what truly frightens me. If I fail, if I do not help James and Holt escape, guards will come for them tomorrow. They will be dragged in chains and hauled over to the scaffold at the town square. The thought sends a pang of anxiety down my throat.

From outside, the jail appears quiet. Torches burn on either side of the entrance. Two large iron rings are propped against the dark, worn wood of the doors. I straighten my posture, tug at my dress to remove the wrinkles, and take a deep breath. I lift one of the rings, feeling the rough, rusted iron scrape against my fingers. I knock twice. The door opens a few inches and a gruff-looking bearded man with a glass eye peers out at me. The warm waft of air that comes through hits my nose with a trace of something rancid, and I repress a grimace. His gray hair falls disheveled to his shoulders. He blinks a few times and then straightens, opening the door the rest of the way. He bows. "Your highness."

I lace my hands together, hoping he won't notice how badly they are shaking. "The king has sent me to retrieve the two servants accused of treason," I say, keeping my voice calm and steady.

The jailer eyes me with a creased brow. He scratches his neck, throwing a glance behind him. "Your highness," he stammers, "forgive me, but you must be mistaken. His majesty has ordered they be executed early morning."

"He's realized these men are the only link we have to the spy living among us. He wishes to interrogate them personally."

The man stares at me with his one, able eye, and I can tell that he is not convinced.

"Well, go on then, go fetch them," I add with feigned impatience.

"But your highness, would his majesty not send the guards for them instead?"

As the words form in my mouth, I already feel terrible. But

it's the only way. "If you question me *one* more time, I will go back to my father and ask him for your head."

His eyebrows rise in surprise. He immediately dips his head. "Forgive me, your highness, I—I will bring them out straight away. Please, come in and have a seat." A mix of guilt and relief burrows into my chest. I silently pray that no harm comes to the jailer because of this.

Inside, the sharp smell of bodily waste permeates the clammy air of the jail. I stifle a gag as I quickly put a hand to my nose and mouth. Thick grime covers the jailer's garments. He gestures to a ramshackle, uncomfortable-looking chair. It sits next to a table where a deck of cards is spread, along with a couple of burning candles, and a sleeping, pudgy man.

The jailer shoves him briskly awake. "Get up, Jackson!"

Jackson awakens red-faced, his eyes and mouth open, disconcerted. He starts mumbling unintelligibly but stops short at the sight of me. Then he scrambles to his feet, pushing his chair back in a loud screech as it scrapes against the uneven, stone floor. He bows his head, almost losing his balance in the process. I find myself smiling at this, though neither of them see it as my hand covers the lower half of my face.

"Come Jackson," the bearded man says, pulling him by the arm. "We've got prisoners to fetch for the princess." Together, they recede into the shadows of the hallway, keys jingling in their grip.

Waiting proves to be very difficult, and not because of my nerves as I would have expected. The stench is overwhelmingly sickening. My stomach churns. I try to focus on the faint echo of dripping water. I can't imagine how anyone gets used to this.

I bolt upright when I hear the clatter of chains and footsteps. The jailers emerge from the dark hallway with James and Holt, their hands bound by cuffs attached to their wrists like pincers. A ball and chain wraps around their ankles. I see surprise and relief on their faces when their uncertain gazes find me. I press my lips tight to sweep away the smile that almost breaks free.

"You may release them," I say with an air of command.

The gatekeepers exchange a glance. Then the bearded man speaks up. "Y-your highness, if they try to escape—"

"They won't escape. The guards have been alerted. They will be closely watched." I swallow. I can feel the sweat building on my temple. The pain in my hands reminds me that I am too tense, that I am squeezing too hard. I am all too aware of the glaring loopholes in my story, of how suspicious it must sound. But I am counting on my title to give me the leverage I need to pull it off. They are my subjects, after all.

I can tell the jailer is thinking it through. I can't let him reason it out.

"I'll take them from here," I say curtly.

He consents with a sharp nod, fumbling with the key ring in his hands. Jackson tries to help him isolate the right key but this only aggravates him, and he barks at him to back off. After several grunts and groans, he manages to find it. He twists the key into the cuffs and chains. I am anxious for him to finish, as though at any moment someone will come bursting through the door to stop me.

When he does finish, however, it's all I can do not to grab the servants and rush out the door. I focus on carrying out the plan. It can be done. I am so close. They are almost free.

I clear my throat. "The king requests an audience," I say to James and Holt. "Follow me." Jackson hurries to open the door for me. James and Holt will remain in the dark until we are in the clear and I can explain myself. I know they will follow me though, confused as they are. With a fervent prayer that we make it to the stables without getting caught, I walk out into the shadows of the night.

We race to the stables like ghosts, scooting along the generous cover of the dark. Reluctant to stop, I give them the details in breathless whispers.

"What will happen to you?" Holt asks in a small voice, his eyebrows glued together.

I stifle a grimace. That's the last thing I want on my mind right now. "Don't worry about me," I assure him through hushed breaths. "I'm the princess, remember?" He smiles a wavering smile, but doesn't say anything else. I offer a confident nod, squeezing his arm.

Guards are posted at several lookouts atop the wall. We dart below them, watching our every step, making sure we do not alert anyone to our presence. We have to be careful; a simple twig or dry leaf is enough to give us away. But tonight the Maker is on our side. Or so I think. We reach the stables undetected. I am practically gulping down relief, as though I've been holding my breath the whole time and I can just now breathe. But my breath catches as we enter the stables. A guard and a servant girl are tucked in the shadows, kissing. They flinch apart at our entrance. For a moment, they seem suspended.

But then Holt's hands are suddenly around my neck, clammy and soft. "Come one step closer and I will wring her neck!" he warns hoarsely. I know his true intentions; I'm not afraid. They are unarmed and thus stand no chance against the guard. His only choice is to bargain for my life.

The guard pushes the girl behind him, drawing his sword. He poses for attack, ready to charge. But he's young. The stubble on his chin hints at a beard that is not quite ready to grow. Breathing hard, he clutches at the handle of his sword, his hand quivering with anger. He must be trying to figure out if he can get to me before Holt breaks my neck.

James stands beside Holt and me, breathing fast in fidgety silence. Every moment that passes feels dreadfully long. What if someone comes in looking for the guard missing from his post? What if one of the stable boys returns for something he forgot? So many other things could go wrong, and as it is, I am doubtful we will be able to haggle out of this predicament.

Then the guard pipes in. "If you do not release the princess at once, it will be *your* necks in trouble." He stares at them like an animal eying its prey, thirsty for blood. If he decides to attack, James and Holt will have no choice but to defend themselves, and they will be slain.

"Please," I say to the guard. "I beg you, do as they say. Put down your sword, *please*," I say hastily.

When the hunger in his eyes falters, I conjure the most grief-stricken expression possible. I would add tears for effect, if only I could muster them. I mouth the word please.

At this, I notice a change in him. Then, like an answered prayer, he lowers his sword, kicking it away from him. He spreads his arms to his sides in cautious surrender.

James crouches for the sword and gingerly picks it up, his eyes never leaving the guard. A sheen of sweat glistens over James' brow. His chestnut hair is slick, sticking to the side of his face. Holt releases me, whispering an apology in my ear.

Holt orders the guard to the back of the stables, pausing to reach for a rope that hangs wrapped around a rusted nail on a supporting post. James follows. They retreat out of view into one of the stalls, leaving the servant girl. She looks to me and back at the stall. Through the shuffling of hay, I can hear the muffled grunts of exerted effort. "He won't be harmed," I assure the girl.

"You're helping them escape?" she asks in a quivering voice.

I nod. "I am. So you must forgive me if I ask you to remain here until they have gone."

"Your highness, I don't want to be involved in this. The king will have me executed—"

"So don't involve yourself," I say.

In the second stall on the left, Daisy, the large caramel-colored mare strapped full of provisions stands ready.

"Hey beautiful," I whisper, stroking the strip of white that runs down her nose, appreciating the softness of her shiny coat. I will miss her. For many years, she has been a constant companion in riding lessons. She is the gentlest of creatures, the tamest of the group, which is why I prefer to ride her over any other horse.

I gently tug at her bridle and she obeys, stepping forward. When I bring her out, I find that James and Holt are ready. They stand side by side. "Her name is Daisy," I tell Holt. "She is yours now. Please take good care of her."

I pet Daisy's nose and give her a small kiss. "Good-bye, darling." Then I turn to them. "Do you have a place to go?"

James nods briskly. "Yes, your highness. I have family up north. They will take us in."

"I'm glad to hear it. Here," I say with a smile. I hand Holt the rolled piece of paper sealed with the blood-red stamp of the crown insignia.

"Show this to guards at the gate but *do not*, for any reason, hand it to them, not even if they ask—which they shouldn't; they are instructed not to. The seal means you're on official business of the king." Holt examines the paper. At their hesitant silence, I press on. "Do you understand? You must be confident. You cannot let them see you are nervous." I point to the letter. "With that in hand, you are above any questioning or suspicion. They will have no reason to doubt you unless you give rise to it."

James responds with a series of quick nods. "Thank you, your highness, I shall never forget your kindness."

Holt's face goes slack, his eyes dull. He looks at me as though he has a thousand things to say, but instead he pulls me into a hug, his arms wrapping tightly around me. A lump rises in my throat and I feel my eyes pool with tears.

"Say good-bye to Beth for me, would you?" he says in my ear. I nod, squeezing my eyes shut to keep the tears from spilling. Holt mounts first, grabbing hold of the reins. Once James is settled behind him on the saddle, Holt gives me one last look, attempting a smile that doesn't quite form. I lift a heavy arm to wave a farewell, and watch them trot off to what I hope will be a long and peaceful life.

Chapter Seven

I can't sleep. My eyes are heavy, they burn with exhaustion, demanding rest. But despite my continued effort, I remain awake. Alert. I don't know how long I waited outside the stables. An hour at the very least. But the night remained quiet and peaceful, without commotion, or the sounding of alarms, which meant that James and Holt were successful at the gate. All I can do now is pray that they make it safely to their destination. Though that is not the only thing that troubles me. Soon, my father will find out what I've done. What will he do? No matter how much I try to brush off the feeling of dread, I cannot will my body to relax. Before I know it, the sun is crawling up through the balcony. Not long after, Anabella waltzes in, carrying two buckets of water for my bath.

"Rise and shine—oh, you're awake." I must not look too good because she makes a face. "Are you ill?" she asks, resting the buckets on the floor. She comes up the side of my bed and touches my cheeks and forehead with the back of her hand.

I shrug. "I couldn't sleep."

Suddenly, the doors to my bedchamber burst open. Two guards and Ulric, the palace chancellor, charge inside. Anabella jumps back, a hand to her chest. "What is the meaning of this?" she demands, her face creasing with concern at what I see, too— the leather whip in Ulric's hand.

He ignores Anabella. "Princess Meredith," he says. "You have defied the wishes of King Edgard.

Fear cripples me, making me weak in the stomach. I knew I would be punished, but I had expected something more along the lines of a slap and a month's confinement. I never thought Father would have me beaten. It will scar me for life. I've seen the backs of servants who were lashed by their masters. Anger floods my vision, making everything blurry. Bile rises and burns my throat. If he wants this done to me, so be it.

The two guards come for me, and though Anabella protests, trying to block their way, she is shoved aside by one guard while the other drags me out of bed like an animal bound for the slaughterhouse. I stand before Ulric, a short, bald man with a pointed nose, and am glad to look down on him. Defiance comes out of me in waves.

"If you truly want me to suffer, I suggest you let someone else try their hand at the whip," I say, arching an eyebrow. Ulric's mouth twists with displeasure. I smile, feeling quite satisfied that I've slashed his confidence.

Ulric jerks his chin at the guards and immediately they are on me, whirling me around and pushing my shoulders down, forcing me to kneel. They tear my nightgown open to bare the skin on my back.

When the first lash comes down, it takes every ounce of me not to scream. The pain is excruciating—stinging, burning, pulsating pain. Tears well in my eyes but I refuse to cry. I clench my teeth and tighten every muscle in my body. Anabella is wailing, crying as if it's she who is being lashed. One of the guards has to hold her back. The lashes keep coming, cruel and unrelenting. It's unbearable. But with every lash, my anger grows. If there was any part of my heart that beat for my father, it is gone now. Stripped away along with the skin on my back. Inside I am snapping, recoiling, swelling with hatred and resentment at each strike of the whip.

Eventually, Ulric's arm tires and the lashing ceases. The skin on my back has become a canvas of raw pain .

"The two jailers who helped you last night were beheaded

this morning. Now, if you'll excuse me, your highness, I have other business to attend to," Ulric says evenly.

This is my true punishment. Jackson and the other man, whose name I never learned, are dead because of me. In saving the wine bearers, I sealed the fates of the jailers. This however, unlike my back, is a wound that will never heal. I will carry it with me to my grave.

And to my surprise, I laugh. My back aches as my sides shudder, but I laugh. I must sound like a lunatic. Ulric and the guards pause on their way out. Anabella comes to me and I am still laughing. My stomach is hurting now. My hysterics echo through the room, and then I'm weeping, weeping for the dead and the living, as everything I've been holding in comes rushing out.

After two weeks of being confined to my rooms, simmering with hate, I am ready to face the world again. Though I walk through the palace with my head held high, I have yet to come to terms with my guilt. I keep thinking of how I could have done things differently. But a part of me knows that no matter what, Father's punishment would still be the same.

At the grove, I find Connor practicing with the bow. A crumpled sack lies by his feet. Bright-red apples spill out of its mouth. Bowstring pulled taut, he stands motionless, eyeing his target. I had wanted to enjoy the grove in solitude, but there is a part of me that is pleased to see him. All the isolation must have gotten to me.

"How's the cold?" Connor asks, shooting the arrow.

I blink at him. "Cold?"

He takes in my expression with a degree of suspicion. "King said you were ill."

I expected everyone to know of my punishment, for Father to announce how he put me in my place for crossing him. But no, he has kept it a private manner. Perhaps he is embarrassed to admit that he was defied by his own daughter. Whatever his reasons, I am glad everyone is ignorant of it. If they didn't like me before, they would surely hate me if they knew it was me who released the prisoners.

"Oh. Yes. I was ill," I stammer, feeling awkward.

Connor angles his head to the side. He doesn't believe me. But just because he knows it's a lie does not mean he knows the truth.

"Show me how," I say abruptly.

He questions me with a raised brow.

I point to his right hand, which grips the bow. "To shoot," I say smiling. A purely meditated move, but to my defense, I *am* curious to learn.

My request seems to surprise him. He stares as though I have found a crevice in the thick, impenetrable wall that seals him closed.

A deep wrinkle settles on his brow. "Why?"

"Because I want to learn," I point out innocently.

"This isn't knitting or drawing."

I scoff. "I am not the kind of girl that is interested in either of those things." I stomp right up to him, tug the bow into my hands, and yank an arrow out of the quiver holstered on his back. I am secretly thankful that he doesn't show any resistance.

Planting myself where he stood only a moment ago, I attempt to shoot the arrow. But while struggling to nestle the arrow on its rest and pin it to my fingers on the string, it falls from my grip and tumbles into the grass at my feet.

Flushing, I quickly crouch to grasp the arrow and spring back up, making sure to avoid glancing in Connor's direction. *Graceful*, I think. *Be graceful.* As a princess should be. Doesn't everyone say grace runs in royal blood? I must be adopted.

I try again. This time I am more successful at resting the arrow on the bow. I clumsily wrap my free hand on the butt of the arrow, smashing the soft white feathers that adorn it. I have no idea how you're supposed to hold the darn thing; I've never been close enough to an archer in action to observe the small details. My mind is already thinking ahead, realizing that if I am lucky enough to shoot the arrow, there is no chance that it will be even remotely close to hitting anything. But I am already here, bow and arrow clumsily in hand. I might as well give it a try.

Squinting, I scan for an easy target, something close and large. A tree trunk would be the obvious choice. But then I feel a pair of arms and hands reach around me, guiding me. I freeze, stiff as a board. Almost enveloped in Connor's arms, I smell the woodsy scent of dirt and dried leaves.

He lifts and bends my arms. "Hold steady," he says, his breath tickling my ear. I find myself unable to focus, distracted by the foreignness of his touch, which seems to be affecting my pulse.

I feel the callouses on his fingers as he adjusts my hold over the arrow. "Now pull the bowstring back, like this." His fingers tangle over mine and I let his strength push our hands back, pulling the string until it can't stretch any further.

"Find your target." Hands at my hips, he slowly pivots my torso. My cheeks burn. When he stops and holds me in place, my eyes find the apple, neatly set atop a thick branch. He releases me and I hear him take a step back. Now, with nothing to distract me, I easily target the lonely apple that dares me to shoot.

"Wait," Connor says suddenly, throwing me off kilter. Startled, I lose my grip on the arrow and it shoots from the bow, completely off target. I am about to look back to see where it's landed, but the severity on Connor's face stops me.

"What is it?" I ask, worried.

His fingers pry at the back of my dress. I spin out of reach, but it is too late.

"Who did that to you?" he asks, incredulous.

I swallow, dropping my eyes, unable to meet his gaze. A humiliating heat burns my ears.

"So this is the *illness* the king was referring to?" he asks, his voice rising.

At my silence, his hand gently takes my chin, guiding my face up, forcing me to look him in the eye.

"Why did he do this to you?" he says in a low voice that brims with anger.

"I helped James and Holt escape," I say finally, giving in to his demanding stare.

I watch as the tightness in his eyes fades, replaced by a softness that flutters in my chest.

He is about to say something when we hear Beth call out. "Meredith!"

She comes our way hurriedly, a hand at the back of her head to keep her cap in place.

"Hey," she says, out of breath, resting her hands on her knees. "I've been worried about you. Why haven't you come down to see me?"

My gaze flicks to Connor, who eyes me with a glint of interest.

I give Beth a big hug. "There is much to tell. Come, let us go for a walk."

Chapter Eight

The following day, I stand before the tall, gilded mirror in my dressing room. The rich blue ball gown, lined with small beads of pearls, complements the shimmering gold under-dress that runs through the bodice. I twirl around, pleased with the perfectly snug fit.

Beth clasps her hands together. "It's beautiful."

"It's perfect," I add, forcing a smile on my face. Though I love the dress, I am dreading the ball. Not only do I hate dancing, I'm not ready to share the room with my father, let alone the same table. I have not seen him since the funeral. Frankly, it wouldn't trouble me if I never saw him again.

"I knew you would like it," Anabella chimes in, buoyantly

pleased.

Beth smirks. "Careful now, you might outshine your infamous dance partner."

It takes a moment to register what she said. "Elijah? Are you suggesting I dance with that beef-witted wagtail?" I snort, thinking of the one and only pebble in my shoe.

Beth frowns. "Don't you remember?"

"Remember what?" I ask, examining the intricate diamond-patterned embroidery on the blue fabric of the dress.

"Elijah won the tournament," Anabella says reluctantly.

I spin around to face them, almost losing my balance from the weight of the whirling skirt. I had forgotten all about it. So he won, after all. I feel the shake of my disapproving head. I'm not surprised. How am I supposed to dance a whole piece with the prig when I can't even stand to be around him for more than a second?

"Well isn't that just peachy?" I mutter under my breath.

Anabella lets out a loud, exhausted sigh. "It's just one dance, my lady."

My lips pucker with distaste, but I keep quiet. It is indeed just one dance.

"After what you did for me, and for Holt, a dance with Elijah should prove a rather easy endeavor, don't you think?" Beth asks. A smile tugs at the corners of my mouth. My dear Beth. In spite of losing her mother, here she is cheering me on so that I can get through a silly dance.

"Think of it this way," Beth continues in a chirpy, encouraging voice. "Once it's over and done with, you will have the rest of the ball to dance with whomever you please."

"You say that as though dancing is an entertainment of choice," I quip.

Beth crosses her arms. "If I remember correctly, you always dance with Charles at royal functions."

That is true. But it's only because I can never refuse that adorable face of his."

Though admittedly, Charles will be a nice reprieve from dancing with Elijah. Then, before I even realize it, my thoughts turn to Connor, and I imagine us whirling across the dance floor. I shake my head. What is the matter with me? I don't even like him. And he doesn't like me. And I am absolutely certain he is not the sort who enjoys silly things like dances. Besides, even if he does like to dance, it's not like he would want to dance with me. Maker, I can just see myself, tripping all over him while he slices me up with those judging eyes of his.

A few hours later, I make my way to the piano room a little early to warm up; it's music lesson day today. Sir Orvin, my music teacher, is always on time. Never early. Never late. He began teaching me when I was nine. I started lessons not understanding a single thing about music, constantly frustrated and hating everything about it. It was a headache. With time however, I came to love the piano, and gradually I improved. Once I became proficient, Sir Orvin's lessons tapered off. Now he comes to see me only once a month, bringing a new sheet of music with him each time, a challenge he dares me to master.

When I come in, I notice the piano fallboard is up. Has someone been playing? The music room is nestled within the west wing, the private area of the palace. It's unusual for anyone besides myself, Sir Orvin, or the maids to come into this room. A piece of paper neatly laid on the piano bench catches my eye. It's a note.

Oblivion awaits at the evening stroll.

As if it were poison, I drop the note, take a step back, and watch it fall to the plush, crimson carpet.

It's a message meant for me, no doubt. No, not a message. A riddle. But I don't have to decipher it to see it for what it is: A warning. The paranoia that strangled me after Geneve's death comes rushing back, clenching my throat. Is the note's author still here? My gaze lingers on the long, draping red-and-gold curtains, pulled back to collect at each side of the sunlit window.

With a hard swallow, I nervously make my way to them. I hold my breath and thrust a hand on them, pressing them against the wall. There is no one there, and I can breathe again. I peer into the hallway, my eyes searching fruitlessly for a guard. They're rare in this wing, as Father prefers his privacy. Someone knew I'd be here today. It's not impossible for a courtier, one who is sly enough, and quick. Is this a cruel idea of a joke? Or am I really in danger?

I pick up the note and look at it closely. The cryptic words and neat penmanship hint at an educated writer. The paper feels worn, as though it has been crushed in someone's hand or pocket for a prolonged amount of time. Its edges are soft and frayed.

I jump at my tutor's voice.

"What's this? No warmup exercises today?" He waits by the door, wearing a knowing smile. Papers—music sheets—stick out from the pile he clutches against his chest.

"I...no. I'm afraid we'll have to cancel the lesson sir."

"Oh," he says with some disappointment. "Is everything all right?"

"I have to speak to someone. It's rather urgent," I say, apologetic.

He taps a finger to his lips. "Would that someone be the vigilant lad out in the hall?"

"Is there a guard out there?" I ask, sure that I hadn't seen anyone on my way here.

"No, the ill-tempered gentleman with the scar on his face."

I give a relieved chuckle. "Yes. That would be him."

I find Connor just as Sir Orvin described him. He paces around, scrutinizing the corridor with those hawk eyes of his.

Wordlessly, I reach for his hand and stuff the crumpled note in it.

He stretches the piece of paper out and reads. His eyebrows knit together. "Where did you find this?"

"The music room—on the piano."

"Did you see anyone besides your tutor?" I shake my head.

"The room was empty."

He brings his hands to rest at his waist. There is an inherent confidence to the sharpness of his jaw, and I find his unkempt, carelessly tousled jet-black hair charming. Even the scar that runs down the side of his face is unusually appealing. It suits him. I struggle to imagine what he would look like without it. But that's where I stop myself, because this kind of noticing makes me feel like a stranger in my own skin, apprehensive of the curiosity he sparks in me.

When I yank myself back to my senses, I notice he is deep in thought, considering something with a frown across his face.

"What?" I ask.

"Do you ever take evening walks?"

"No," I say, thinking of the time I spend at the grove, either alone, or with Beth or Charles. Come to think of it, I've never set foot in the grove after dark. Not that it scares me—or anything of the sort—it's just not proper for me to be out so late.

He nods as though that was the answer he was expecting. "Either way, you should refrain from the courtyard and the grove until we have an answer."

"Even in broad daylight?" I ask, not pleased with the idea.

"Yes."

I scoop the note out of his hand and point an indignant finger at the word evening.

He snaps the piece of paper back into his possession. "It's a *riddle.*"

I fold my arms across my chest. "And your point is?"

"It's figurative."

"What else could evening mean?" I ask with a shrug.

He takes a deep breath and holds it. "It could mean many things, or nothing at all; it might be there to mislead." He pauses to glance at the note again. Then he folds it up and digs it in his pocket. "I'll walk you to your rooms."

"What are you going to do?" I ask, trailing after him.

"Your father needs to be informed."

My feet come to a stop. "No," I blurt out, louder than I intend to.

"Why not?"

Let's see. I'd rather kill myself than ask him for his advice, let alone his help. "I just...I'd rather not."

Irritation settles in his eyes. "This isn't up for discussion."

My hands twist and fidget. "He...I don't believe he has my best interest at heart."

Connor leans in with a commanding air. "The urgency of this threat exceeds your quarrels with your father. He will do whatever it takes to keep you alive."

The knock on my door abruptly tears my attention from the yellowed pages, though frankly I am eager to close the book; there's only so many hours of embellished poetry I can endure. Connor greets me when I open the door, looking peeved.

"May I come in?" He asks.

I step back, pulling the door the rest of the way.

"Refreshments?" I ask.

He declines with a shake of his head, taking a seat on the chaise. For a moment, he examines the cover of the old book lying next to him.

"Your father is increasing security," he announces.

"That's good," I say with a nod, taking a seat beside him. "But why don't you tell me what is bothering you?"

He rakes a hand through his hair. "He refuses to believe any-one in his court could be involved. And your uncle agrees with him."

"Yes, well, it must be easier to believe that when you're not the one being threatened," I say, my voice laced with sarcasm. "But there will be more guards around, right? And then there's you, lurking around corners and tree branches."

For a moment, he eyes me with a twinkle of amusement, but he quickly lapses back to his normal, inscrutable self.

"Whoever wrote that note will expect all of that," he says.

I chew on my lip. How does one anticipate the moves of a murderer when they don't make any sense?" Why bother to write the note? Why take a chance at us solving the riddle when he can simply barrage me into oblivion whenever he pleases and be done with it?

He shrugs. "Maybe the furtive attack is not his style. If this is the same person who poisoned your drink, then it's probably someone who is after the thrill of a challenge. There were plenty of other opportunities to poison you, but he waited for a public display."

I feel my mouth run dry. "Why kill me in the solitude of my rooms when he can do it with an audience?" I say, almost in a whisper.

"Which means this *evening stroll* is not something you will do alone," he says.

"That," I start. "That sounds like someone who's insane."

"He probably is," he admits, glancing over at me, a trace of apprehension in the set of his jaw.

"But wouldn't we be able to tell if there was a madman in our midst?"

"I don't think we're dealing with that kind of lunacy. This is someone who is intelligent and calculating. He could be any-one."

I sigh, pretending like it doesn't rattle me. "I guess we'll find out soon enough, won't we?"

Chapter Nine

I gape at myself in the mirror. "I look like a jester."

Bright-red pigment covers the sides of my ghostly powdered face. Anabella was so enthusiastic about trying the assortment of colors and shades she purchased at the market that I could not deny her. Although, I have to admit, I was curious to try them myself.

Anabella sweeps me over with a strained smile. "Yes, it does seem a bit...eccentric. I think I got a little carried away."

"*A little?*"

She pours water from the porcelain pitcher sitting on the dresser onto a cloth. "Here. Wipe it off."

I scrub vigorously, folding the cloth over and over as it becomes saturated with red. The skin on my face tingles from the friction. When I look back in the mirror, I've almost gotten it off.

"Let's try this again," she says, dipping the brush back into the powder.

I put my hands up. "Let's not."

Her lips pucker into a pout. "I'll do it right this time. I promise."

"No, that's all right. I think I'll be more comfortable without it." If previous balls are any indication, most of the ladies will be prancing around with painted faces, though nothing so excessive as Anabella has fashioned.

She drops her shoulders with a sigh. "As you wish, my lady."

"We can practice some other day," I say. "We can invite Beth—she would love it. And you'd have two faces to practice on." I beam at her, hoping to assuage her disappointment.

Accepting the offer with a small smile, Anabella helps me into my gown. She spends a good while pulling on the strings at the back, tightening them to the point where I can barely breathe. I grip one of the bedposts to keep from flying backward. When she is satisfied with the fit, she proceeds to fix my hair with pearled pins, the sound of distant music echoes through the walls into my sitting room.

The ball has begun.

My palms sweat. I briskly rub them against the dense fabric

of my dress. All day, I've avoided thinking about it. But with the music whispering in my ears, I can no longer ignore it. Apprehension stirs in between my ribs. Anything that involves dancing makes me nervous, especially when every eye will be pinned on me. *And let's not forget your dancing partner.* But I am lying to myself if I think that is the only reason why my palms are sweaty. *Oblivion.* I hear the word echo in my head. Nonexistence; death. Although Connor's constant presence is comforting, I can't help but feel paranoid that there is someone out there, waiting for the orchestrated moment to strike.

I force my fretting feet to be still against the marbled tile. I listen to a whole three pieces by the time Anabella is done. "There," she says.

My locks of hair are elegantly pinned atop my head in a style that suits me like a crown. I commend her with a wide grin.

"Does my lady approve?" she asks, clearly pleased with herself.

"It's stunning. Thank you," I say, clasping her hand.

A startled look comes over her. She turns my hands over to wipe my palms. "Is something the matter?"

Oh, it's nothing. Just some madman on the loose who wants to kill me. I do want to tell her though; the words hang at the tip of my tongue. But confiding in her now would only make things worse. She will most certainly panic. And as I'm bordering on panic myself, that's the last thing I need right now.

"I'm just a little nervous about the dance is all."

She hugs me from behind, smiling at my reflection. "Don't fret, child. You will be wonderful."

At the ballroom entrance, a pair of guards open the large, gold-embossed white doors. The merry sound of violins and cellos flows through the vast room, resonating against the walls and the chandeliers that dangle from the high ceiling. Tall Corinthian columns line either side of the elevated entrance hall where I stand.

Alongside me, the Lord Chamberlain blows the trumpet to announce my entrance and the music comes to a stop. The stairs are gallantly decorated with a wide crimson rug, and in the sea of guests, the buzz of conversation dissipates.

"Princess Meredith!" calls the Lord Chamberlain.

Like wolves on prey, all eyes are on me as I begin my descent down the steps. I stare back at the crowd, fidgeting under my skin. That's when I find a pair of dark, observant eyes. He watches from behind the crowd. For a moment my legs falter, unsure of their footing. I focus on him, as though he is a pillar, guiding me through the wolf's den. It's all I can do to keep my eyes on him. I navigate the remaining steps with alert and steady feet. When I step onto the polished wood floor, the courtiers part, clearing a narrow path for me. As they move away and bow, Father comes into view. I feel the ghost of a throb on my back at the sight of him. He sits on a slightly elevated rectangular platform on his red royal cushion in a golden chair. To his right, a similar, smaller chair sits empty, waiting for me.

My hesitation feels loud in the eerie quiet of the room. Stepping onto the platform, I avoid making eye contact with Father. To my relief, the moment I take my seat, he stands, cup of wine in hand, and walks off into the crowd as people return to their conversations and the music resumes. So neither of us can stand the sight of the other. For once we have something in common.

Tables upon tables of food are set along the eastern wall. Even from where I sit I can smell the salty aroma of smoked turkey and the tangy bitterness of pickled vegetables. Despite the growl of my empty stomach, I am too weary to think about eating. I would probably end up vomiting all over the place. A servant appears before me, carrying a silver platter with several cups of wine. My frayed nerves scream enthusiastically at the sight of alcohol. But then, as I smile at the servant for a cup, he hands it over to another servant, who takes a small sip.

Ah, the tasters.

Let's make sure someone else drinks my poisoned wine, shall we? I can't help but cringe, and suddenly I no longer have a desire to drink. But if the servant just risked his life for me, then the least I can do is follow through. I have just gratefully grasped a cup into my hand when it is roughly taken away.

"I would strongly suggest you refrain from consuming any food or beverage this evening," Connor says.

"It was tested," I say, frowning.

"Just because there are no immediate symptoms doesn't mean it isn't poisoned."

"Well, I guess I wouldn't put it past a crazed man to have more than one kind of poison," I mutter.

I notice he's dressed in the formal attire of a soldier—a fine, double-breasted uniform, navy blue, flawlessly tailored to his strong arms and athletic build. I recognize the golden lion's crest stitched on the left shoulder. The crest of Alder. The sight of it dusts the cobwebs off a question in my head.

"Do you know Ethan? The prince?"

The question seems to still him. He studies me and I feel suddenly absorbed into the void of his probing eyes.

"What do you want to know?" he asks after a moment.

"Is he...decent?" I ask, gingerly.

"Don't worry. He's nothing like your father."

The words are an immense relief. All my life, I've worried that I'd be married to a man who would make my life miserable, a man incapable of kindness and affection. But that isn't my only concern. Ethan is a prince, royalty, which probably means he is insufferable.

"Will I like him?" I don't know why I'm asking. It's not like he could really know the answer to that, observant as he is.

He answers straightaway: "Yes."

"Really?" I ask, half-smiling.

Before anything else can be said, the music stops short, followed by Father's dour voice.

"Esteemed guests. We are gathered here today, on this festive occasion, to honor our country. Our land. To honor our kingdom. But as you all know, we have recently lost one of our own. I would like to take a moment to honor her and her family with a toast." Father raises his cup. "For Lady Geneve and the House of Bacchus. Tonight we promenade in your name."

Everyone commemorates Geneve and her family. Without a cup in hand, I can only bow my head in respect.

"Promenade?" I hear Connor mumble under his breath, brow wrinkled in a deep frown.

"Is something wrong?" I ask, reaching for his arm.

He looks at me then, and the expression on his face lifts the hair off my arms.

"The evening stroll," he says, his voice taut. "It's the ball." Before I can react, I feel a sharp tug at my shoulder.

Charlotte is glowering at me, her face as red as a ripe tomato. "Who do you think you are?"

It takes me a second too long to clear the fog in my head and understand her meaning. Before I can answer, she is digging a bony finger onto my chest. "How dare you disrespect her like that? It's you who should be dead. You are alive thanks to her. And you can't even make a toast in her honor?"

"I didn't have a cup to toast with," I say, hoping she will be rational in spite of her anger.

Charlotte breaks into a menacing cackle. "How convenient. Others might believe your lies, but I see right through you; I know the truth. You knew the king would make a toast in her name. You *knew*. And you made sure you would be empty-handed, didn't you?"

My eyes widen with disbelief. I shake my head. I'm not sure if she actually believes what she's saying, but if she was trying to make a scene, she would be yelling at me, or at the very least raising her voice enough for those close enough to hear. But then, I notice the glistening in her eyes and the shaking of her hands. This is not for show; she's convinced of her own words.

"You carry on, pretending to be so innocent. You want everyone to think you are *so* good. But you are rotten. Wasn't it enough, killing our queen?"

The unexpected words ring like thunder in my ears. "What did you say?" I ask, slow and cautious.

This seems to catch her off guard. She flashes me a mocking smile. "You didn't know? You killed your own mother. Giving birth to you made her sick. Are you that thick? Why do you think the king hates you so? How could he forgive you? How could any of us? You killed our queen. You took away his beloved."

I feel as though she is grabbing hold of my heart with her hand and crushing it in one swift squeeze. I want to punch her and yell to the world that she's a liar, but for all my confusion, all the rage storming inside me, there is only a single tear, slipping down my cheek.

"No. That isn't true," I mumble, more to myself than to her. Or was it? Did I really kill my mother?

"Yes it is. You're a murderer. You have blood on your hands," she says.

"Enough!" Connor growls from behind us. Surprised, Charlotte spins around to face him. He glares at her with undeniable violence, as though he could strangle her with his eyes. She takes a step back, her hands slightly raised in defense.

"What's going on?" I hear a warm voice ask. Charles. I feel his gaze on me, but I can't bring myself to look at him.

"Your sister needs to sit down," Connor tells him.

Charles, who knows too well the animosity between Charlotte and me, does not hesitate to ferry her away.

"I killed my mother," I whisper, incredulous. "Is that why he hates me?" I wonder, thinking of my father, my eyes trailing to him out in the crowd.

Connor stands right in front of me, demanding my attention. "Get it together; this is not the time to be falling apart." The words hit me like a slap, bringing me to my senses. And I feel my body go rigid as a slicing fear chops my insides into mush.

To stroll, to promenade; a ball.

Connor is about to say something else when the Chamberlain's trumpet blares.

"Ladies and Gentlemen, it is time for the first dance. Please make way for Princess Meredith and Sir Elijah Gannon!"

Applause booms in the ballroom like thunder. The ovation sounds more like a warning. The dance could not have come at a worse time. I look over at the entrance doors and consider making a run for it. I could blame it on my nerves. I could say I did not feel well and suffered from palpitations.

But then Elijah is before me, looking devilishly handsome in all-black attire. Surrounded by guests garbed in color, he stands out like a regal thumb. He glances curiously at Connor, then he simply outstretches his hand. "Your highness," he says, smiling wickedly. "May I have the honor of this dance?"

I'd rather rot, I want to say, but I give him my hand anyway. Walking through the sea of parted guests, I force myself to smile. At the very center, a large circle has cleared. As we approach, the musicians begin to play the slow, rhythmically cheerful sound of Stonefall's traditional dance. In one slick motion, Elijah twirls me around in his arms. He moves with steps that never fail to confuse my feet. I know the moves by heart, but the message gets lost in translation to my legs. I do my best to follow along. Step, step, twirl. Step, step, forward. Step, step, switch. I manage well enough. Getting through an entire dance without stumbling or stepping on Elijah's feet will be a victory all in itself. I just need to focus.

"You are an odd little bird, princess," Elijah says, watching me with curious eyes.

I can't let him distract me, or I will lose my concentration. It's my duty to dance with him, but there is no reason why I need to humor him.

He laughs at my silence, a laugh of true enjoyment, as if my aloofness pleases him.

Twirling me to his side, he says, "You absolutely cannot stand me, can you?"

Surely he doesn't need me to answer that, does he? It's like asking me if the sun rises in the morning.

"That's why I like you," he says, winking at me with an impish grin.

I bite my tongue to keep from lashing out at him. It's too bad there's not a step in the dance that calls for a knee to the groin.

After another two or three gruesome minutes of dancing with Elijah, the piece comes to an end. We bow our thanks to the excited audience. When the musicians play their next piece, guests giddily flock around us to dance with their partners. Eager to get away, I pull my hand free of Elijah's grasp. Except he doesn't release me.

"Dance with me again." His smiles as though challenging me to accept.

"No," I say emphatically. I pull my hand again, but with his iron grip around it, it doesn't even budge.

"Please?" he asks in a honeyed voice, a stark contrast to the force with which he pins me in place. "Just one more dance. I won't ask ever again. I promise."

I frown at him. "I don't think you realize that dancing is not my strong suit."

He laughs, throwing his head back.

I roll my eyes. "I am not dancing with you again, Elijah." I gesture at the ballroom. "This room is full of ladies who would love to dance with you. Why don't you ask one of them?"

He shakes his head. "I'd rather dance with you. And I'm not taking no for an answer." At that, he hooks an arm around my waist and spins us around. I glare at him, feeling trapped. I could attempt to pull away, if only to make a statement, but that would only cause a spectacle. I want to dance my worst and step all over him, make him regret wanting to dance with me. But I am a coward; I am too self-conscious of the embarrassment that would bring.

Amid the steps and turns, I catch a glimpse of Connor. His eyes are everywhere but on me, keeping watch of my surroundings. I also find Charles. His sister is nowhere near him. Our eyes meet and he tilts his head, a questioning smile on his lips. *Are you all right?* It seems to ask. I attempt a smile and hope it's enough to ease his concern.

"I really do like you," I hear Elijah say, but I ignore him. Instead, I shift my attention to the struggling movement of my feet.

"I did warn you, princess. You should have listened. But you could not figure it out, could you?" he says, pausing to observe me. By now he has my full attention. Warnings flash in my head but I am stranded in his arms. "I must say I am bit disappointed. But I was right; you have no idea how much I love being right. Though I would like you to know, it's nothing personal."

He gives me a triumphant grin as a sharp pain radiates at the back of my waist. He bends down to place a light kiss on my cheek. "Sweet dreams."

The room blurs as he walks away, weaving through the dancing couples. There is a dizzying haziness in my eyes that I can't blink away. The music seems to have suddenly slowed to a distorted crawl. I feel numbing pain at my waist, and something wet. Vaguely, I can make out my fuzzy hand. Covered in red. Blood.

Charlotte's words echo in my head. *You're a murderer. You have blood on your hands.*

The ballroom spins and I stumble backward. I hear a muffled scream. Commotion stirs around me but I am falling and I can't see anymore, as though I am being dragged away from it all in some black tunnel, farther and farther away, until the screams become whispers.

Chapter Ten

As I come to, the pain sharpens. Opening my eyes, my room comes into view. My lips are dry, sticking to each other. My throat feels as rough as pumice. I swallow, but with a parched mouth, it does little to soothe my discomfort. On a small table by the window is a glass pitcher, full to the brim with the clearest, freshest water I've ever laid eyes on. Not thinking twice about it, I move to get out of bed. But as I lift my torso, pain shoots up like needles, jabbing and stabbing with spiteful stings. I gasp, lying down against the comfort of my pillow. I hold my breath until the pain ebbs to a bearable sting.

I gently push down the covers to my legs. I don't have to lift my nightgown to see the blood-stained bandage wrapped on my skin. It curves over the whole left side of my waist. Then I remember. The dance. Elijah. *He did this to me?* The young champion of Stonefall? It just doesn't fit. Sure, he is pompous and vain, but a murderer?

It's nothing personal.

Recalling the events of the ball, I remember the confrontation with Charlotte and what she said about my mother.

Then the door opens. Anabella pops in, her hands busy with something, as always. She carries a dark-brown leather bag.

"You're awake!" She scurries over to me, plopping the bag by my feet. She is quick to touch my forehead." Maker's gate! Your fever has gone. How are you feeling?"

"Like I've been stabbed." I sound so hoarse it's as if I haven't uttered a word in days. "I could use some water."

"Oh, yes, of course," she says, scrambling over to the pitcher and pouring me a cup.

I drink the water in greedy gulps. It goes down, cold and revitalizing, at once erasing the cotton-mouth feeling in my throat. I end up drinking another two cups before my thirst is quenched.

Anabella brushes some of the matted hair out of my face. "We almost lost you, child. It's a miracle you're still alive." That's when I notice the dark, puffy circles under her eyes. And I could swear there are new wrinkles on her face.

"I'm sorry," I say, feeling guilty for being such a constant source of grief.

"Don't apologize. This wasn't your fault," she says, tenderly rubbing my cheek. "You're safe now. That's all that matters."

"What happened last night? Was Elijah caught?"

"Last night? Child, you've been slumbering in fever for the past two days," she says. "But no, Elijah escaped the night of the ball."

This I was not expecting to hear. "I don't understand. The room was full of guards. And Connor was there. How did he get away?"

Anabella shakes her head. "Connor went after him, but guards stopped him."

I frown. "Guards? Why?"

"It seems they were working for Elijah."

A knot forms at the back of my throat. Members of the guard. The very men on whom I rely for protection. Men I trust with my life. Working for the enemy. How do I know the guard outside my rooms won't swing the door wide open for Elijah when he returns to finish me off?

"Wait. What did you mean the guards stopped Connor? Is he all right?"

She smiles, as though I've said something funny. "Oh yes. He suffered a bruise here and there, but he's as healthy as a spring chicken."

I let out a relieved sigh. "What happened to the guards?"

"Three of them are dead. The other two are under interrogation. From what I hear, they refuse to answer any questions; they will likely have to be tortured for information."

My face twists into a grimace. Torture. I push the thought away quickly.

"It's time to change your bandages," Anabella says, changing the subject. She pulls linen and a jar of honey out of her satchel.

She takes off the bandage. "The wound has closed. But you have to be careful not to open it up again."

I nod, holding back a whimper as she smears the healing gash with honey.

When she finishes, she places the items back in the leather bag. "Now, why don't you rest some more? Your body needs it. I'll be back in a little while with a warm bowl of soup."

"Anabella..." I trail off, twisting the threaded cotton sheet of the bed between my thumbs. "Did my mother die from giving birth to me?"

A knot of deep wrinkles creases between her thin, gray eyebrows. "She died from illness, do you not remember?"

"Yes," I say, nodding. "But I was told that she got sick because of me."

"Who said that to you?" she asks, incredulous.

"Charlotte."

"Ugh. That poisonous cow. You should know better than to believe her. The queen was practically glowing when you were born; I'd never seen her so happy. She was healthy for a good couple of months before she started showing signs of illness; it had nothing to do with you. So get that dreadful idea out of that pretty little head of yours, do you hear?"

Though her answer is what I wanted to hear, there is something else that lingers in my chest, unresolved. "What about my father? Is that what he believes?"

She presses her lips together in a sympathetic smile. "Your mother's death took its toll on the king, but I am sure he does not blame you for it."

At that, I almost pity Father. It's sad that I find it hard to imagine him as a loving person. "Was he an agreeable man back then?"

Her face strains for an answer. "I believe he is still the same man he was when your mother was alive." My nose wrinkles as though her words smell foul.

"And my mother loved him?"

"He was different with her," she says. "He must have really loved her. Everyone else around him was no exception. Not even family." She trails off, pensive, as if remembering something. Or someone.

"You can say that again," I mutter.

"You may think he's hard on you, but the king is capable of much worse." She trails off, pensive, as if remembering something. Or someone.

"Hard on me? He *hates* me. What could possibly be worse than a father who doesn't love his only child?"

She pauses, tugging at her bottom lip. Finally she sighs and says, "I'm not supposed to talk about this, but I suppose there is no harm in sharing it with you…your father had another brother. An illegitimate brother. His name was Theodore. Your grandfather was very fond of him, but your father and uncle were not. They shunned him and refused to accept him as their brother. And when your grandfather passed away, your father took the throne and banished Theodore from the kingdom; he was escorted to the border and left to fend for himself." She shakes her head, her gaze cast down. "He was just a boy."

I lean back, appalled. Illegitimate or not, he was family. How could Father throw him out like that? "What became of him?"

"No one knows. But then again, the king forbade anyone from speaking his name." An uncomfortable swallow runs down my throat. I feel surprised, despite my low esteem for Father. A small part of me had held on, refusing to give up on him. But I cannot believe that is the case now.

"Now, you be a smart girl and keep any mention of Theodore out of your father's ears," she cautions as she moves to leave.

"Anabella?" I ask, before she can open the door.

"Yes, my lady?"

"Don't go. Please," I say, shrinking at the thought of being alone.

"Don't you worry," she says with a warm smile. "Connor's keeping watch in the sitting room."

"Oh."

I catch myself smiling, surprised at the elation that bubbles out of me. I shake my head. I just want to be safe. And I feel safe when I'm around him. So clearly I should want to be around him as much as possible.

I wake up to sounds of a hushed argument.

"You expect me to leave you two alone? In her bedroom?" Anabella says to someone at the door.

"Yes," Connor's voice replies. My eyes fly open.

After days in bed, I know I look a mess.

"She's not yet awake sir," Anabella points out.

"I'll wake her. It's important."

Running a hand over my hair, I cringe at the coarse, matted mess that I am certain will require several hours of combing to fix back into shape. I sigh inwardly. So much for trying to look decent.

Anabella raises her chin at him. "Then you will have to tell her in my presence."

"It's all right, Anabella. I'm awake. He can come in."

Anabella opens the door the rest of the way and scowls at me before stepping aside to let Connor in. Standoffish, arms crossed, he waits for Anabella to leave. She mutters under her breath, shaking her head as she stomps off to my sitting room, slamming the door behind her.

Not seeming to care, Connor crosses the room in a few quick strides, taking a seat on the empty chair next to my bed.

To my relief, I'm not the only one who looks disheveled. An angry bruise discolors his left temple and dark circles of sleep deprivation shadow his eyes. He looks like he hasn't shaved in a few days, but I must say the stubble suits that rugged appeal of his. His exhausted gaze lingers at my bandaged waist. Has he rested so little to keep watch over me?

"I'm sorry," he says.

I shake my head. "You don't have to apologize. Anabella has her outbursts, but she—"

"No. You got hurt because I failed you."

Understanding his apology, I see guilt written all over his face. He feels responsible. Is that what's kept him from resting? But it wasn't his fault. No one would have expected Elijah to be the attacker. A need to reassure him swells in my chest.

"You didn't fail me," I say softly, resisting the urge to reach for his hand.

He looks me straight in the eye. Beneath the exhaustion, I can sense a burning defiance. "I failed you," he insists. "It is not up for discussion."

"Fine," I say, throwing my hands up. "So what is it you wanted to tell me?"

"With palace security compromised, we have no way of telling how many others were recruited. And your father doesn't know anything." He tells me the last bit with an audible tinge of distaste.

I nod. "Yes, I figured as much when Anabella told me what happened. But what about the two guards you captured? Are they not being questioned?"

Connor shakes his head. "All we have managed to get out of them is that they work for Theros. They'll be tortured to death before we can get anything else of out them."

So Elijah works for Theros, too? And to think he's been living among us for years. Had he planned to kill me all along? I frown. It sure is an awful lot of time to set a plan into motion. How can he be so loyal to a madman? Then I remember Elijah is a madman himself. I wonder if more of his men might lurk in the halls of the palace. What I am supposed to do now? Lock myself up in my rooms for months?

Then, as if reading my thoughts, Connor says, "I can't protect you here."

Is he leaving? "What are you saying?"

"You're coming with me to Alder."

My pulse quickens. Alder. He's taking me to Alder. "When?"

"As soon as you are able to ride a horse."

I can feel my nerves coming apart at their seams. I knew this day was coming. I knew that I would say good-bye to my old life. But not so soon.

"But it isn't time yet. I'm not supposed to—"

"Elijah failed; he might be willing to forego the theatrics and take a more direct approach next time. The king is pressing efforts for guard replacements, but he doesn't have the manpower to do it all at once, it will take time."

I rest against the headboard to quiet the sudden dizziness that spins in my head. "Connor, I can't marry the prince—not yet— I'm not ready."

He quirks an eyebrow. "I'm not taking you to your wedding. This is about your safety."

"But won't the prince demand to marry me once I'm there?"

"Does it say anywhere in the marriage contract that the date of the wedding can be changed?" he asks.

I pause for a moment, recalling the verbiage of the contract. I've read it about a thousand times now. I remember the dread I always feel from just holding the paper in my hands.

... two weeks hence from her 18th birthday, Prince Ethan Caster of Alder and Princess Meredith Holbeck of Stonefall shall be wed...

"No. I don't believe so," I finally admit.

Even with that reassurance, I still feel averse to the idea of traveling to Alder. At least it will give me time to get acquainted with the kingdom. And the prince. After all these years, I will finally get to meet him. I look up at Connor and recall him saying I will like him. I hope, for my sake, that he's right.

"Did my father agree to this?"

He nods. "Besides you and me, he's the only one who knows. You cannot tell anyone else we're leaving or where we're going," he says.

I understand the importance of secrecy. But the few people I trust? "What about Anabella? And Beth? What about my cousin, Charles? You cannot expect me to leave without saying good-bye."

"You must," he repeats.

In an instant, his eyes set with that uncomfortable intensity, wordlessly demanding my acquiescence. Under the beguiling stare, I feel a conflicting mix of attraction and rebellion stir within me.

"I can trust them," I say, refusing to agree.

"No," he says. "That knowledge might put their lives at risk.

If anyone suspects they have information, they will go to any lengths to get it out of them."

I open my mouth to disagree. But I stop myself. He's right. I have to protect them.

"You do realize Anabella will raise hell when she finds I've disappeared?"

"The king will send for her before that happens," he reassures me.

"Wait," I say, as an idea lights up in my head. "Could Beth and Anabella come with us?" I would bring Charles too, if only he could come. But his place is here. At least he is the son of the duke, and he can afford some protection.

"No. We must travel through the Borderlands. If we get into a bind, I can't guarantee their safety. You are my priority. If it comes down to it, I won't risk your life to protect them."

The Borderlands. The land of the lawless, or so it's called, commonly known to be dangerous territory for foreigners, as there is no actual law to abide by. It's the stretch of land that leads to Alder, enclosed by the Telinnor Mountains. Its fertile soil produces two thirds of the wheat consumed in Stonefall. The land has been a constant source of political tension between the two neighboring kingdoms. But two hundred years ago, in an effort to encourage prosperity and good relations, the king of Alder decreed that neither kingdom would control the land and allowed for free trade, provided no one ruler ever claimed sovereignty over it. Thus, the people of the Borderlands were exempt from taxes and regulations, boosting demand and increasing their profits. To this day, it has proved to be a successful sanction; trade between the Borderlands and its neighbors continues to flourish. But it's far from a perfect place. With no ruler to command the land and provide order, its growers are vulnerable to robbers and pillagers. A group of outlaws formed, calling themselves the Borderlords. They extorted the people in exchange for protection, lest their fields be burned and their homes ransacked. The people of the Borderlands had no choice but to pay. The only benefit is that foreign robbers are deterred, and crime remains low. That has proved reason enough for Alder and Stonefall to turn a blind eye to Borderlord extortion.

"What will become of Anabella?" I ask. "She was supposed to accompany me to Alder. I can't trust my father to do right by her when I'm gone."

"We can send for her—and your friend—once you are safely settled. Alderian guards can escort them safely across the land."

"Fine," I concede. Requesting a royal entourage to escort a chambermaid and a servant seems a bit outlandish, but left with no alternatives I can only hope Connor is right.

Chapter Eleven

My Dearest Cousin,

I've just heard the news that your fever has broken. I will finally be able to sleep soundly tonight. I still cannot believe what Elijah has done. He sure knows how to ruin a girl's dress, does he not? In all seriousness, I am eternally grateful to the Maker for thwarting his plans. To think I considered him a friend turns my insides out. Perhaps next time I should pay closer attention to those you dislike. We have much to catch up on. But I'm afraid that will have to wait. My father has some business to attend to *with the Count of Wakefield, and he has requested I accompany him. I shan't be gone long. I promise I will pester you as soon as I return.*

Your most favorite cousin,
Charles

Charles' optimism is contagious even on paper. But the smile he brings to my face is bittersweet. Even if the business that has called him away is brief, Wakefield is a fortnight away on horse-back. I will be well on my way to Alder by the time he returns. I decide to leave him a letter explaining myself—as much as I can—without divulging any crucial information.

Beth visits as often as her duties allow. If she didn't have to sneak up to my rooms, she could manage much easier. But as the days go by, it becomes harder and harder not to say anything about Connor's plan. On several occasions, as Anabella happens to speak of things we'll do once I'm better, it almost slips out. I do my best to bury the guilt and enjoy my time with them as much as I can, knowing it could be months if not years before I see them again.

On Connor's orders, I remain inside my rooms despite my

improved condition. In the meantime, I try to prepare myself for the changes that are to come. No longer will I sleep in my bed. No longer will I be able to take afternoon walks at the grove, or visit Beth in the evening after a long day of mentally exhausting social events. This life, the only life I have ever known, is about to end. An unknown, uncertain future awaits me. I suppose I might as well embrace it with open arms. At the present, however, there is still plenty of healing to do. But confined to my rooms, there is only so much reading and pacing I can do.

Today I feel so bored that even a game of chess sounds exciting. I remember I keep a set in my sitting room. I think for all the years it's been there, I have only played it twice, with Charles. The first game was a total disaster. I played not really knowing what I was doing, and according to Charles, I lost miserably. I blamed it on beginner's bad luck. The second game was an attempt to redeem myself; I never picked up a chess piece again after that atrocious play.

Maybe I could play a match or two with Connor. I might even get him to open up a little. That's if I can even convince him to play. He asked not to be bothered while he keeps watch; he wants as few distractions as possible.

Undeterred, I waltz into my sitting room. Connor springs up from the white linen couch.

"What's wrong?" he asks.

I was worried he'd run himself sick keeping constant watch, but he looks rested.

"I'm bored," I say.

He gives me the raised eyebrow but says nothing.

I blow air on the neglected chess board and its pieces. Dust billows. I cough, feeling the scratchy particles in my throat. "Sit down with me to play some chess. You've played chess before, have you not? I must warn you though, I am terrible at it. You might have to take it easy on me."

I feel his eyes on me as I tread over to the table, balancing the game with my hands. I let it drop gently onto the surface and slide into one of the chairs. I look back over at Connor, who is now resting an elbow against the wooden mantelpiece.

"I said no distractions," he says, dryly.

"And like *I* said, I'm terrible at chess. You can probably beat me with your eyes closed. It's hardly a distraction."

He cocks his head to the side. "If you're so bad at it, then why do you want to play?"

"Because right now it sounds more appealing than staring out the window." I gesture with my hand for him to join me. "Now let's play some chess."

Connor comes over, petulantly taking the open seat across the table. I feel victorious already.

He lifts his chin, gesturing for me to make the first move.

"You must be happy to be returning home early," I say, pushing a white pawn forward.

He nods, moving a pawn.

"Do you have family there?" I ask, moving another pawn.

He seems to think it over for a moment before answering the question. "No. My parents are dead." He pushes the piece with the horse.

I use a pawn to take down one of his. "And you have no brothers or sisters?"

"My aunt is the only living relative I have left, but she doesn't live in Alder." He uses his horse to take down my pawn.

"Hey, that's cheating! You can't move your horse piece sideways," I protest.

His mouth twitches. "You mean my knight? You really are bad at this, aren't you? The knight can move horizontally and vertically," he says.

A subtle heat makes its way to my cheeks. "It's a horse. Why is it even called a knight? It makes no sense."

For a second, I think I see the hint of a smile on his lips. "I didn't make the rules."

"In that case, I hereby declare this piece 'the Horse,'" I announce, holding up the piece. Then I steer the conversation back to Connor. "So your aunt, where does she live?"

"The Borderlands," he says, seizing another of my pawns.

"She owns land there."

"Really? Isn't that dangerous? For a woman, I mean."

Connor stares at the board, planning his next move. "My aunt is not your typical woman. She has plenty of hired help, too. And she has the support of her neighbors; they're like family, they look out for each other."

Watching his moves, I try to follow along, moving my pieces in similar fashion. My bishops and horses take center stage, defending my side of the board. I position one of the castle pieces to the left side of the board. Connor shakes his head.

"What?" I ask.

"You want to keep your stronger pieces at the center."

"Oh," I say, feeling silly. He moves his hand over mine to guide me, placing the castle back where it was and then moving it forward, taking one of his own pawns. I silently order the obnoxious flutters in my stomach to go away.

Several moves later—in spite of Connor's helpful instruction—I've lost most all of my key pieces, save for the queen, a castle, a few pawns, and of course, my king. I realize I am about to lose the game.

"I am curious to know how you plan to get us out of here without being noticed," I prod. "There are guards everywhere."

He captures my queen. "There's a secret passage behind the king's rooms; it will lead us outside the palace walls. Someone will have a horse ready for us there."

Secret indeed. I almost ask why it is that I had no idea of its existence, but then I remember whose secret passage it is.

"Oh," I manage to say.

Then he moves his queen into just the right position; I have no move.

"Checkmate."

The next morning, I fold the note and place it neatly by the orchids. In it, I explain to Anabella why I had to leave in secrecy, trying to be as reassuring as possible. I promise to write to her as soon as I get to my mystery destination, hoping it will help ease those mad nerves of hers. I also ask her to personally deliver the notes I leave for Charles and Beth. Connor waits for me by the door to my rooms. With bow and quiver slung across his back and two short swords in scabbards, he looks like he's about to head off to battle. I, on the other hand, don the simplest piece I own, a gray linen dress I used to wear on Father's hunts. Though it's not practical for travel, at least I am not burdened by the usual heavy layers of fabric that come with the more formal gowns in my closet.

"Are you ready?" he asks.

I give my room one last look. "Yes," I answer a little shakily.

We move side by side at a hurried step, neither running nor

walking. The west wing is calm as usual, and though there is no one around, I still feel imaginary eyes at my back.

There are new guards posted at Father's door. They look young and uncomfortable underneath the metal breastplates, lacking the confident air of the guards before them. They move to let us in without question. Inside, Father waits on one of his chairs, a cup of wine dangling lazily from his hand. He takes a sip, regarding us with a cool stare. Of all the things that crossed my mind ever since Connor spoke of leaving, saying good-bye to my father had not been one of them. My double-crossing heart winces at the realization. I'd been preoccupied with the idea of leaving home, and everything else it entailed, except for this. Will I ever see him again? Father peels himself off the chair.

"I expect King Perceval will send word to me once she arrives?" he asks, though it doesn't really sound like a question.

Connor doesn't give him the satisfaction of a straight answer. "He may."

Father's lips press into a thin line.

"You make sure that he does," he says with thinly veiled impatience. Then he directs his scrutiny towards me. "And as for you, daughter, do not make a fool out of me in their court. If you ever do anything right in your life, let it be that." He smiles, but the gesture is unkind and filled with resentment. It takes every ounce of me not to cast my eyes down. I jut my chin at him.

"Is that all?"

He ignores the question, dismissing me with a scowl. "You will have your hands full trying to keep that girl safe," he says, turning to Connor. "But you do well to remember what is at stake here, soldier. I cannot afford to lose her."

"She is in capable hands now, your majesty," he replies, nonchalant, as though he didn't just insult the king. My eyes bulge out of their sockets. Father arches a miffed brow. But to my astonishment, it isn't followed by a lashing outburst. Father takes another sip of his wine, seeming to drown his anger in it.

"Let us get on with it then," Father announces.

We follow him into his bedroom. Red walls and golden curtains border the spacious room. A chandelier hangs low, shining light into the four post bed enclosed by a set of embroidered, maroon drapes. Father stops before a tapestry on the wall, depicting a hunting scene of a pack of dogs attacking its prey of deer. He lifts the heavy fabric, revealing a narrow, knob-less door etched on the wall. He pushes it open with the press of his palm. Connor motions for me to follow Father so he can take the rear.

Inside lies a musty, downward-spiraling corridor, shrouded in darkness. A torch burns ready at the entrance. Father takes it with his free hand, the cup of wine sloshing in the other, and leads us down the precarious steps. The space is small enough that I can rest a hand on each side of the damp walls, steadying myself as I go. I feel the silky threads of split cobwebs under my fingers, and I resist the urge to shake myself.

In spite of Father's comfortable and acquainted gait, he moves at a crawling speed and I am able to keep up with him. At one point, however, my foot pinches the hem of my dress over one of the steps and my hands slide away from the guiding walls. My body pivots forward, but before I can tumble onto my father's unsuspecting back, a hand clamps on to one of my flailing arms, holding me back. I balance a skidding foot on the next step down and regain my composure.

"Thank you," I whisper breathily to Connor, who reluctantly lets go of my arm, skeptical of my stability. Thankfully though, with a hand lifting my dress, I manage the rest of the way without any more slip ups.

We are greeted by an ancient-looking iron door. Father wheels to face me, shoving his cup into my hands, droplets of wine splashing onto my fingers and chest. Then he digs in his pocket, procuring a large, single key. He slips it into the keyhole, the metal groaning as he turns it. The door opens with a loud, scraping sound and light comes flooding in, blindingly bright and almost painful. I squint. The figure of a man on a horse waits outside. As my eyes adjust and the details of his face become more discernable, my lips curl into a silent snarl.

The chancellor.

He sits on a familiar black stallion. The landscape of rolling hills behind him suggest we are at the northern wall of the palace.

"Your majesty," the Chancellor says with a bowing head at Father. Then he smiles at me. "Your highness."

"Get off my horse," Connor demands in a calm but warning voice. Eyes wide, the chancellor's mouth falls slack, clearly not used to being told what to do by anyone besides the king. He hesitates, throwing a glance at my father, as though expecting a response from him. But as Father keeps quiet, the chancellor finally dismounts, stomping down on the grass with a high chin.

Connor approaches the horse. The majestic creature greets him with a nudge of its nozzle.

"Provisions have been packed for the two of you," Father says, his eyes pointing at the leather pouches strapped to the saddle. "Use them wisely. Now, if you will excuse me, I have other business to attend to." He gives me a brief nod and then treads back through the door, the chancellor darting behind him, jamming the heavy door shut. The turn of the lock echoes like a good-bye of its own, final and irrevocable. I pretend as though it doesn't bother me.

So long, Father.

"You remember Princess Meredith, don't you boy?" I hear Connor ask the horse.

"Does he have a name?" I ask, grateful for the distraction.

"Diago."

"Hello again, Diago," I say, petting his long, shiny neck. "How long have you had him?"

"Nine years," he says without thought. "I was eleven when my father brought him home." A rueful expression pales his face. But in a second, he is back to himself. After he checks all the knotted ropes carrying our provisions, he hoists a foot into the stirrup, using his arms to lift his body up on the saddle.

He offers me a hand. "Come on."

Ride with him? The entire way? The skin on my cheeks warms like an oven. "Why can't I ride my own horse?"

"Must you always ask so many questions?"

I scoff, fisted hands at my waist. "Must you always refuse to answer them?"

He exhales loudly. "Having you on another horse is less secure for both of us. Now will you please take my hand?"

"There. That wasn't so hard, was it?" I ask but he ignores me. I take his hand, stepping on his foot for leverage. He pulls and I huff my way up, hanging on to his shoulders for balance once I swing my leg over to the other side. Gingerly, I circle my arms around his waist, pretending to be nonchalant about it, as though my blood does not course with a nervous thrill. As I press my body against his back, Connor works the reins, digging his heels at Diago's sides. The horse momentarily lifts his two front hooves off the ground and takes off like an arrow, slicing through the wind.

I look back, unable to help myself, and watch as the palace, the only home I've ever known, disappears behind the hills.

Chapter Twelve

I play with the silver spoon, scooping up a spoonful of porridge and watching it fall back into the bowl in thick lumps. Up until the moment we were served, my stomach had been growling with hunger. But when I laid eyes on what the inn people call porridge, my hunger was chased away to the pits of Talos. To make things more appetizing, we ended up at the only empty seats of the long dining table, next to an old man who wishes the entire inn to hear him slurp.

"Eat," Connor says from across the table.

"I'm not hungry," I say, avoiding his eyes. Instead I comb the dimly lit dining area of the inn. Dirty walls that—I am assuming—used to be white, encompass the modest room. The place is as full as a festival banquet, except there are no flashy tapestries; no lavish performers, no haughty, overbearing courtiers prancing around. And most definitely no banquet delicacies from the palace kitchen. Everything appears to be covered in a grimy layer of dirt and grease. I quickly realize etiquette is not a common practice among the guests, as I hear the loud, drunken banter travel through the stuffy room, accompanied by the occasional belch. To have arrived here after an exhausting day on horseback was not the most rewarding experience, though I am relieved to be off the horse. I did not realize how much my back and legs ached until I dismounted. The few stops we made along the way were not enough to give my limbs rest.

I hear the heavy clink of the spoon as Connor drops it against the rim of his bowl.

"Eat anyway," he commands.

I wordlessly push the bowl in his direction.

He studies me for a moment before pushing the porridge back to me.

"I'm still not hungry," I say, crossing my arms against my chest.

He stares at me, looking like he's about to reprimand a child. "You need to eat."

Eating nothing but an apple and a loaf of dry bread while traveling on horseback for almost an entire day is hardly enough nourishment, so yes, I do need to eat. I gladly would. I would eat like a ravenous beast. If only there was some decent food around here. I look down at the uneaten bowl of mush before me. With an exasperated sigh, I shove a porridge-loaded spoon in my mouth. But just as I begin to chew, my tongue registers a trace of spoiled milk among the mushy grains, and my face twists into an involuntary grimace. My first instinct is to rid myself of the foul food, but not wanting to spit it all out in front of Connor, I hastily chase it down with a large swig of Connor's ale. My deprived stomach churns ungratefully. Disgusted, I wipe my mouth with the sleeve of my dress.

"I can't," I say, still recoiling from the bad taste in my mouth. "It's awful."

Connor nods, taking another spoon of his porridge. "Awful sounds about right."

Just watching him eat it, now that I know what it tastes like, is nauseating. And the sloppy, unpleasant slurps of the man next to me don't help.

Gulping what is left of his ale, Connor stands. "Let's get our rooms," he says.

Connor speaks to the innkeeper at the front desk. "I need two adjacent rooms."

The innkeeper's glasses slide down the bridge of his nose as he peers up at Connor from behind the desk. An unusually long white beard drapes down his chin, resting on the ledger he holds in his hands.

"I don't have any adjacent rooms available," the innkeeper says grumpily, adjusting his glasses with his index finger.

"Do you have any across from each other?" Connor asks.

The innkeeper shakes his head.

"In the same hall?"

Again, the innkeeper shakes his head.

Connor runs an impatient hand through his hair. "Do you have *any* rooms?

"Yes, I have plenty. Shall it be two, then?"

When Connor doesn't answer, I shoot him a sideways glance. From the hard set of his jaw, I can tell he's not too happy with the innkeeper's sarcasm. But after a moment, he seems to collect himself. "One," Connor says.

The innkeeper reaches for the quill on his desk, shaking the excess ink back in the bottle.

"One room?" I ask Connor, thinking I must have heard wrong.

"Yes. One," he says, not looking at me.

The innkeeper, who had paused, quill in hand, resumes to jotting something down on his book. He then unlocks a drawer, procuring a key.

"Room twelve. That will be two silvers," he says, handing the key out to Connor.

After Connor pays, we make our way to the back of the inn and look for room number twelve. At the entrance of the hall, we see a pair of doors, the first with a number one etched on the flimsy wood of the door, the one across it with a number two. We round a corner at the first end of the hallway. I can't help but notice that as the numbers increase, so does the heat at the top of my ears. By the time we find room twelve, they are scorching. How does he expect me to share a room with him? I want to say something, but when I open my mouth to speak, I choke on my words. Connor, seemingly unfazed, wastes no time turning the key in the lock. He pushes the door open, revealing a room that's much too small, fitted with a single, dingy window donning a pair of pale blue tattered curtains, furnished with an uncomfortable-looking bed, a small desk table and a chair. There is one other door, which must lead to the bathing room.

Hesitant to step inside, I remain rooted at the door, my hands gripping the frame.

"Please come inside," Connor says.

Taking a couple of skeptical steps, I slowly close the door behind me. But the moment I do so, the awkwardness of the situation grows tenfold. I stand uncomfortably, rubbing a hand against my arm, and pretend to be fascinated by the hideous pattern of roses on the curtains.

"Look, I know this makes you uncomfortable," he says. "It's not exactly easy for me either. But I must keep you safe. We'll just have to make the best of it, all right?"

I nod, having never felt more embarrassed in my entire life. And I've had my fair share of embarrassing moments. But never something like this. I'm surprised the skin on my face isn't melting off from the maddening heat that flows underneath it.

"You can have the bed. I'll sleep on the floor," he adds.

I glance down at the dusty wooden boards. Next to that, even the bed looks comfortable. "Are you sure?" I ask, feeling selfish. There's no way I'd be able to sleep with him lying right next to me, but I don't think it's fair for him to sleep on the floor. Besides, he needs his strength more than I do.

"Perhaps it should be me who sleeps on the floor," I offer.

Connor shakes his head. "Don't worry, I won't have trouble sleeping on the floor. I've done it many times before. But I'll steal one of the pillows, if you don't mind."

I smile. "I don't mind. I'm not big-headed enough for two pillows anyway."

And then he smiles at me in return. It's a small smile, insufficient but also genuine. A smile that makes my mouth run dry. I don't think I've ever seen him look more handsome. It's too bad he doesn't smile more often. Then again, that might prove too dangerous around me. As it is, I'm worried I've developed more than a fancy for him. But that can't be. I'm betrothed to the prince, and it's not like I have an exit clause out of the marriage. My heart has no business wandering.

When the sun begins to set, Connor lights the candles by the desk. I take one of them with me to the bathing room so I can slide out of my dress. Looking down at my chemise, I curse myself for not bringing a coat. But it's not like I could have expected to end up in these sleeping arrangements. As I wrap my hair into a side braid, my stomach growls, reminding me that I have yet to eat. I would rummage for something from our provisions, but they are barely enough to get us by for the next few days. I'll just have to wait until tomorrow. Hopefully breakfast will be edible.

When I come out of the bathing room, Connor is already set up on the floor with one of the pillows. I notice he is still wearing all his clothes, save for his boots, arm guards and jerkin, which hangs on a hook, and I am suddenly very conscious of myself.

I am considering shutting the door and slipping my dress back on when Connor says, "I'm not looking." I shift my gaze in his direction and find he has an arm over his eyes. Not waiting for him to take a questioning peek, I hurry to the bed, silently chastising all the rickety noises it makes, and pull the sheets over me.

"You can look now," I say slightly out of breath.

Without a word, Connor gets up to put out the candles. Not bothering to use the candlesnuffer, he pinches them with his fingers. Soon after, the faint scent of smoke fills the dark room. Hazy moonlight filters through the curtains.

"Goodnight," I say, feeling a little strange.

"Goodnight," he replies after a moment.

I sigh, shifting over to my side. The bed feels incredibly stiff under me, like a plank covered in fabric. Sleeping on the floor couldn't be much different. Trying to make the best of it, I close my eyes and wait for sleep to come. It doesn't. After several tosses and turns, I'm still lying there, eyes closed but perfectly awake. I had expected to pass out after such a long, exhausting day on the road. But in the quiet of the room, my thoughts turn to home.

Is Anabella struggling to sleep, too? I can't imagine how worried she must be. And Beth. Charles should be on his way home by now. I only just left and I am already missing them. I think about my new life in Alder. What if Beth and Anabella never make it there? What if Father forbids them from leaving Stonefall? What if Charles never visits? I can only reassure myself that I will see them again soon. I have to hold on to that hope.

My stomach, not wanting to take no for an answer, starts growling again. Amid the still quiet of the night, it's incredibly loud. I wordlessly tell my stomach to be quiet, praying that Connor is a deep sleeper.

But then I hear rustling, and I see Connor's silhouette as he gets up, reaching into his bag on the table.

I prop onto my elbows and watch him as he walks over to me. He offers me something with an open palm, but it's too dark for me to make it out. So I take it and lift it up to my nose.

An apple.

"I was saving it for your breakfast, but that hunger will keep you up all night," he says, sitting down on the bed, right next to me.

"Thank you," I say, a little embarrassed. "But why were you saving it? Aren't we eating breakfast here at the inn?"

"Yes," he says, with a ring of amusement in his voice. "But it's porridge again in the morning."

I groan, resting my head against the headboard. Biting into the apple, I push the nauseating thought of porridge away.

"Did I wake you?" I ask.

"No. I can't sleep."

"Neither can I. When did you decide to become a soldier?" I ask, hoping we can at least pass the time with conversation.

"My father decided that for me. He was the captain of the

guard. He wanted me to follow in his footsteps; he began to train me when I was eight."

"Was that what *you* wanted?" I take another bite. The juicy sweetness quickly appeases the hunger, though it will only be a temporary fix. I will have to find something in the morning to keep me going. Anything but that awful porridge.

Connor thinks my question over for a bit. "I don't know," he says, finally. "I was too young then to know what I wanted. I looked up to my father, so I never felt opposed to it."

"Is that how you got your scar? Training with your father?" I ask.

At that, I sense Connor tense up. "No," he says, looking away.

I immediately regret having asked the question. "I'm sorry, I didn't mean to pry," I start.

"It happened the night my mother was killed," he whispers. The audible pain in his voice tugs at my heart.

I put a hand to my face, losing my grip on the apple. But before I can even think to reach for it, Connor is handing it back to me.

"Please, you don't have to tell me," I mumble. Though I am curious, I'd rather not make him relive the memory.

Even in the dark, I can feel those intense, brooding eyes boring into me. "I want to," he says.

I hold his gaze for that moment, unsure of what it makes me feel. I want him to tell me. I want to know more of him, like an odd puzzle I'm determined to solve.

"I was ten years old. My father was away on business at the time, so it was just my mother and I at home that night. After we went to bed, raiders attacked the house, a group of them; I don't know how many. They pillaged the house and killed most of our servants." He pauses, and I can hear him swallow. I sense that he is bracing for whatever it is he is about to say. I open my mouth to tell him to stop, but he goes on.

"My mother told me to hide under the bed. She put up a fight when one of them burst through the door. When I heard her scream, I crawled from under the bed. I didn't have a weapon on me, and I didn't know what I was doing, I was just reacting. He was about to thrust a sword in my mother's chest when I lunged at him, throwing wild punches. I'm not sure how it happened, I was blind with fear and rage. All I remember is the sting of his blade as it cut down my face. He must have backed off, more from surprise than anything. He stared at me with his one eye, but it was too late. He'd already stabbed my mother in her stomach. She died quickly." Connor sounds distant.

A lump lodges in my throat. I can't imagine how hard that must be, and to be reminded of it every time you look in the mirror? I want to comfort him, to wrap my arms around him. But I am not bold enough. Instead, I reach for his hand. I give it a gentle squeeze, lacing our fingers together. He returns the squeeze. I am suddenly too aware of our hands laced together. A moment ago, the gesture seemed apologetic, comforting. And I intended it that way. Now it feels intimate, as though a thousand things could be said through the clasp of our hands. Enclosed in the intense, palpable silence, I hear the loud beat of my heart against my ears. But then Connor pulls his hand from mine, and the moment, whatever it was, is swallowed by the night.

"Get some rest," he says, softly.

He gets up and walks over to the other side of the bed, lying back on the floor.

My mind is racing now, digesting the silent exchange. I try to lay still and piece my thoughts back together, but it's no use. I feel like a stranger in my own skin. As the minutes go by, I feel more and more tired. My eyes are heavy. Connor makes no sound. I shift to my left side to get a look at him. I can make out the slight movement of his head. He's awake. I feel obliged to say something.

"Did you...kill him?" It seemed farfetched, an unarmed, ten year old boy, but how else would he have survived?

"He let me live," he says.

"Really?" I say, in disbelief. "Why?"

"I don't know. Perhaps watching me cry over my mother's

body moved him. He left without saying a word."

"And you never saw him again?"

"No."

"What would you do if you did?"

He pauses. "I pray that I never do."

"Why is that?"

"Because I don't want to be a monster."

When I open my eyes, it feels as though I've just closed them. I can't remember actually falling asleep last night. Even with the shabby curtains drawn, the golden light of day opens up the confined-feeling room. The floor next to me is empty, but the pillow Connor slept on lies neatly against the headboard. I glance over at the closed bathing room door. Is he in there? Then I catch sight of a bundle resting on the table, with a note laid next to it.

Eat & get ready. I'm right outside.

A smile creeps up the corners of my lips as I unfold the white cloth, revealing a flaky, freshly baked loaf of bread and a handful of grapes. Giddy and grateful, I peek my head out the door. Connor rests against the wall to my left.

"Thanks for breakfast," I say, beaming at him.

His lips curve almost imperceptibly to one side, the ghost of a smile.

Not wanting to make him wait much longer, I gobble down my food and rush into the bathing room, happy to find the tub ready for me, filled with clean, clear water. Just how early did he rise? I must have slept like the dead. With soap in hand, I vigorously scrub at the grime that clings to my skin and underneath my fingernails. Once clean, I slip my dress back on. The subtle smell of the muck that rises from it bothers me. The same smell I cleansed off my skin only a few moments ago. The hem, of course, is completely soiled, but that is to be expected.

Ready for another grueling day of travel, I am about to walk out when the front door swings open, its edge slamming against my temple. Seeing stars, I tumble a few steps back, warding off the offending door. I hear Connor curse under his breath.

"I'm sorry," he says. "But we've got problems."

"Don't tell me they ran out of porridge," I say, rubbing at the throbbing spot on my forehead. I come off snappier than I intend; being hit by doors on the face must bring out the sarcasm in me.

But both the swelling welt and my sauciness vanish into thin air when Connor speaks.

"Theros' men are here."

Chapter Thirteen

"How do you know?" I ask, unable to keep the rising panic from my voice.

Connor pushes on the window shutters, but they hardly budge. "I heard them coming down the hall." He thrusts his shoulder at the window and the shutters fly open.

"You *heard* them?" I ask, puzzled. "Did they announce themselves or something?" Aloud, the question sounds as stupid as it did when it popped into my head. But how else would he know it's them?

Connor jumps out the window in one swift motion. He swivels back, holding out his hand for me. "Who else would be looking for room number twelve?" he says quickly.

Propping up a leg, I heave myself up and land in the grass outside.

I cling to Connor's arm under the dry, baking heat of the sun, casting furtive glances at the people around us. I'm not sure what I'm looking for exactly, having no idea what Theros' men look like. I keep expecting to see men in uniform. I lay eyes on a plump man with an unusually long mustache that curls at the ends. Sweat trickles down the sides of his bald head as he wheezes, struggling to lift what looks like a sack of potatoes onto a cart.

Hurrying along through the crowd of people, I narrow down my search to able-bodied men and anyone that looks the slightest bit up to mischief. But among older men and women who seem too preoccupied with their own business, and small families whose children run around in giggles as their parents deal with luggage, no one seems suspicious or out of the ordinary.

As we near the stables, I catch sight of a familiar face. The second I make the connection, my entire body runs cold, as though I've just been dunked into an ice bath.

Elijah.

Connor senses my distress. "What is it?"

Before I can answer, he follows my gaze to the entrance of the inn, where Elijah stands, along with two other men. There are only three of them, which I find interesting, given that Connor defeated five men all at once the night of the ball. Connor must be debating this too, as I notice his fingers twitching around his scabbards, where his short swords are tucked. Then a group of six men comes out to join them. They must have been the ones who had gone inside to track us down. One of them shakes his head at Elijah. That's when he turns to scan the area—and locks eyes with me.

"Let's go," Connor orders through clenched teeth. He doesn't have to tell me twice.

This time we make no effort to be inconspicuous, breaking into a run. My short legs are no match for Connor, who moves in long, fast strides. He practically drags me to the stables.

Connor lifts his thumb and index finger to his mouth and whistles, loud and clear. Not a second later, Diago comes dashing out of his stable, tossing aside the stable boy who had just been tending to him, prepping him for the road. As Connor hoists me up on Diago, I look back, mouthing the word *sorry* to the boy. He blinks back at me, dazed and confused.

Connor swoops up behind me and squeezes his heels against the horse's flank. Diago bolts out of the stables, and my whole body slings back onto Connor. People dodge and curse as we blow past them.

I spot Elijah's men running after us through bewildered onlookers, though the moment they see us galloping away they slow to a defeated halt. Eerily calm, Elijah watches us escape, arms crossed. An icy feeling scurries down my spine. It's as though he is enjoying this, like a game of cat and mouse, waiting for us to hide so he can come pounce on us when we least expect it.

Knowing Elijah will soon be on our trail, we veer off the highway and stay away from inns. After about a half a day of nonstop riding, there is an uncomfortable ache running down the sides of my legs from sitting too long in the same position. The strain at the small of my back returns, though today it's much more painful than it was yesterday, and that much harder to ignore. I constantly shift my weight on the saddle, but I fail to find a better position.

In the late afternoon, we stop for the night in an open area encircled by trees and thick undergrowth, with a large pond in its center. My eyes light up as we come upon it, relieved to see a body of water. I can't wait to soak off the sticky film of dried, salty sweat that clings to my skin. But as we dismount, I hobble over with stiff, sore legs to the water and take in the murky green color, registering a briny fish scent that lingers in my nose.

"There are no other ponds close by, are there?" I ask, deflated.

Diago comes up beside me to drink.

"Don't drink that water," Connor cautions. For a moment, I think he's talking to the horse.

"There is no need to warn me," I say, making a face at the muddy water.

Well, if I can't take a bath, at least I can get some rest, but that hope is also dashed as I realize we'll be sleeping on dry grass. I never thought I would want to get to Alder so badly.

Disenchanted, I walk over to the plushiest grass I can find and plop down to sit, legs crossed beneath my skirt. Connor unstraps the bow from his back.

"What's wrong?" I ask. With plenty of tall, thin-trunked trees and thick bushes between us and the road, the area around us could not be more hidden. There is only the buzzing of cicadas, announcing the sun will soon set, and the occasional breeze that ripples through the trees.

"It's time for dinner," he says. "I won't go far."

"Can't I come with you?"

"You make too much noise."

"And what is our dinner, exactly?" I ask, afraid it will be something exotic, like a toad or a snake.

"I'll know it when I see it," he says with a shrug.

Even though my stomach grumbles with excitement at the thought of meat, I can't help but feel sorry for the poor animal who crosses Connor's path.

"What about berries?" I suggest, hopeful.

"None around here," he says, readying an arrow between his fingers. "Stay here. I'll be right back."

At some point, I doze off, because I open my eyes to the smell of roasting meat and the flickering, dancing light of a small fire. Two squirrels, skewered with a stick, cook over the flames. The sun descends, hovering above the tree line. It will be dark soon. Blinking the fuzziness out of my eyes, I discern a shape coming out of the pond. My first instinct is to get up and run, but then my eyes adjust and I recognize the figure. Connor. Naked from the waist up. I've never laid eyes on a shirtless man before, but taking in the defined muscles across his chest and abdomen, I get the feeling this isn't what the typical man looks like. His jerkin and shirt, bunched up in his fist, drip water as he walks up. I realize my jaw is hanging open like some salivating idiot. I close it. He lifts his head in my direction and our eyes meet. I look away quickly, feeling the singe of embarrassment in my cheeks.

"Water's not so bad," he says, stopping right at my feet.

I nod, making an acknowledging sound in my throat.

"My shirt needs to dry. Better get used to me this way," he says with amusement.

"Good thing you decided against washing your pants then," I say, flushing. With his torso bare, I notice the chain around his neck. There's a silver medallion hanging from it.

"Hungry?" he asks, kneeling by the roasting squirrels.

"Famished would be more like it."

We eat, hovering by the fire. I take greedy bites, feeling better than I've felt since we left. I can't believe I've gone so long, eating so little. But then again, maybe it was the scare we had this morning that gave me the energy I needed to carry on.

"What's that thing around your neck?"

"It's a coin with my name on it, a gift from my mother."

"Do you ever take it off?" I ask, wishing I had a token of my own.

"Never. It's all I have left of her."

"You have your memories. That's what I would fear losing the most—if I had any," I say, almost melancholy.

Connor regards me with interest, quiet and thoughtful. "You are right, princess. Memories are our most prized possessions."

My ears cringe at the formality. "Please, call me Meredith."

"Very well, Meredith." A tinge of hesitation edges as he says my name.

My hands fidget. I clear my throat. "Do you think they'll find us?" I ask, busying myself with my food; taking my last bite. I chew slowly, trying to enjoy it as much as I can before pushing it down my throat. Though I feel fuller than I have since we left the palace, I'm still not quite satisfied, but I resist the urge to lick my fingers. Instead, I wipe them on the stiff, soiled fabric of my dress. My eyes drift back to the pond. Maybe I should take a dip and let the cool air dry me off overnight.

"It's only a matter of time," he says, pensive lines etched on his face.

The thought sends my stomach to the tips of my toes.

"You don't think we can outrun them?"

"We could try," he says. I balk at the casual tone in his voice, as though this is a common topic of conversation to have over dinner. *We might get our throats slit in our sleep. Would you care for more squirrel?*

"What do you suggest we do then?" I ask.

"For starters, I need to put out this fire before the sun sets." He gets up, kicking a load of dirt into the fire. The flames vanish with a hiss and, save for the last rays of light peering through the trees, we are left in darkness. The charred wood that remains lets out a single thread of smoke that twirls up into the purple night sky. I can already feel the chill in the air.

"We'll have to detour; lay low for a while," he adds.

I hope he is not suggesting we live out here in the woods. "Detour where?"

"The Borderlands."

I sit straight up. *Stay* in the Borderlands? It's one thing to pass through there, but extending our welcome for more than a day seems foolish. Hiding out in the woods suddenly sounds wonderful. Even a cave harboring a den of hibernating bears seems like a better plan. "What? That's insane! You know as well as I do those people don't take kindly to strangers. Aren't there, I don't know, safer places to hide?"

"You can't blame them for their hostility; they've had a rough life. But we'll stay at my aunt's, so you don't have to worry about that. We'll be welcomed guests."

It *sounds* like a good idea, but it sure doesn't feel like one; I am not entirely convinced that we should do it. But I have to remind myself to trust Connor.

With both the sun and the fire gone, I consider the idea of bathing without my dress. The darkness seems to provide enough coverage for me to take a dip in the nude. Another benefit of bathing in the dark: I won't have to see the murkiness of the water. That should make the process a whole lot easier.

"I'm going to take a bath," I awkwardly announce when Connor lies down on the grass.

"I would advise against it; nights are cold out here. Why don't you wait until morning?" he asks.

The wheels of my brain turn uncomfortably. How exactly do I explain that I'd rather bathe in the dark so that I can take my clothes off and not worry about him seeing me naked?

"The breeze will dry me off," I stammer.

I dip my foot into the water, and for a moment, I almost

change my mind. It's chilly. It will be a very short bath, the shortest bath of my life, actually. The moment I submerge my body, I come up gasping, shocked at how cold the water is, like the sting of snow when pressed against the skin for too long. I madly scrub my arms and legs with my fingernails, sure that I will leave welts on my skin. But at that freezing moment, I couldn't care less.

In minutes, I am scrambling to get back in my dress, but lacking something to towel off with, my dress is soon thoroughly damp, and when the next breeze blows by, I am left with prickling skin and chattering teeth. I knew I would be cold, I just didn't think it would be this bad. Why don't I ever listen to him? Now I have to walk back there and pretend everything is fine and dandy.

I slump down on the grass. I lie on my side and draw my knees against my chest, clutching my arms around them. And I thought sleeping at the inn was bad. The grass is rigid and scratchy. Though I think I am spent enough to fall asleep on such an unwelcoming surface, there is no way I'll be able to shivering. Hopefully it won't take all night for my dress to dry. But if anything, it will keep me alert to anything approaching. Not that I don't expect Connor to wake at the sound of a feather falling on the ground.

Behind me, I hear Connor stir, the grass crunching beneath

him. I try to be still, but my body is too cold to keep from shaking. It takes me a moment to grasp what is happening when I feel Connor's arm around me. I flinch a little, surprised by the touch. A twinge of thrilling confusion toils within me when I look over my shoulder at him, but as the warmth of his skin radiates through me, thawing the icy coldness, understanding smoothes out my furrowed brow. And I am suddenly overcome with an unexpected tightness in my chest, leaving me breathless.

I wait for a sarcastic remark to remind me of my poor decisions, but all I get is the steady rise and fall of his chest.

"I...thank you," I manage to say.

He squeezes my arm. Not long after that, I notice a change in his breathing as he dozes off. I fixate on it, letting it drown out the synchronized humming of crickets and the incidental hoot of nocturnal birds. When I can finally get over the fact that Connor is holding me in his arms, his rhythmic breaths calm my apprehensive heart. With only the moon and the Maker as witness, I push aside all my inhibitions and restraints, and let myself bask in the safety and comfort of Connor's arms. Before I know it, my body has warmed, and I am drifting off to sleep.

Chapter Fourteen

It takes us another five days to get to the Borderlands. I am beginning to feel like a creature of the forest. At least I'm sure I smell like one. The last few days on the road don't seem half as bad as the first. I think my body has adjusted to the hardships of the road, appetite included. We have consumed all of the bread and fruit that were packed in our supplies, but a bird or squirrel will suffice now, and I have managed to set aside my qualms over eating them, even watching Connor skin their dead bodies and skewer them with sticks.

We've avoided Elijah and his men. Though I am at a loss as to whether this is truly due to chance, or if it is somehow part of his twisted game.

"We're here," Connor says, just as the dirt road begins to widen. Farmhouse silhouettes soon appear on the horizon of the vast, flat land. The bushy terrain gradually changes into lush green fields, marked by rickety wooden fences. Fields of wheat ready for harvest line the road, stretching out as far as the eye can see. People at work speckle the crops. I don't know why I expected a gloomy landscape of withered trees and menacing clouds. The whole atmosphere is charming; sunlight shines bright among the scattered bunches of white clouds, and I can hear the happy chirrup of birds perched on the fences. They flutter away as Diago approaches.

We pass dozens of wheat farms before Connor signals Diago to halt. We come up to entrance of a two-story home made of carved stone. It looms before us, looking dark and impenetrable. Four pairs of small windows lined by bricks encompass the front of the second story, while a porch punctuated by three large arches stands below. At the front is a colorless vegetable garden. Connor navigates Diago away from the road and onto the path that leads to the house.

Just as Connor dismounts, a tall woman, about the same age as Anabella, appears by one of the arches.

A wide smile spreads on her sun-withered face. "Maker's plight!"

She hurries up to Connor, who pulls her into a tight hug, her feet briefly dangling.

"My precious boy, it's been years since I last saw you. Look at you." She takes a step back, her eyes jubilant. "What a fine young man you've become." She speaks with a firm, strong voice that complements the tough manner about her.

A gentle half smile curls the corners of Connor's mouth. "It's great to see you too, Aunt." I watch them with nostalgic eyes, reminded of the affection I yearned for back home.

Then Connor beckons me to dismount with outstretched arms. I rest my hands on his shoulders and he grips my waist, lowering me to the ground. Our eyes meet for a split second, and I notice something in his gaze, a look I can't quite place. But it's there and gone before I can exhale the breath caught in my chest.

"Meredith, this is my aunt, Jessamine Grieves."

"Pleased to meet you, Mrs. Grieves," I chime with a curtsy.

Jessamine quirks an eyebrow, shifting her eyes between Connor and me. "*Princess* Meredith?"

"Is it that obvious?" I wonder if something in my countenance gave it away, because I am certainly not dressed for the part.

"A lucky guess," she says with a shrug. "And please, call me Jessamine." From her casual demeanor, it's evident she has no intention of treating me as a royal. I couldn't be more pleased.

After Jessamine delegates a servant to take Diago around

back, she motions for us to follow her inside. We walk into a dark, compact foyer. The heavy scent of wet bark hangs in the air. The walls, set with small beams, are stuffed with rubblework. To the left is an open door that leads to a well-lighted room. From where I stand, I can see part of an oven, so it must be the kitchen. At the far left of the entryway is a flight of wooden stairs. On the far right, a doorway that seems to be missing a door opens to a parlor. Back against the wall, a fireplace sits directly in the opening's path, dark and unlit.

Jessamine takes us up the rickety stairs to the second floor, where there are four bedroom doors.

"That one there is my room," Jessamine says, pointing at the door farthest to the right. "The other three guest rooms are ready for use. Make yourselves at home. You look like you've had quite a journey, so why don't you get cleaned up and rested, and I will see you both downstairs for dinner." She walks to the door of her room but stops before going inside, focusing on Connor. "Be sure to show her out to the bathhouse, dear." Then she looks over at me. "I'll leave you a change of clothes there."

We both give her a silent nod and she disappears into her room, closing the door behind her.

"Bathhouse?" I ask, trailing after Connor, who is peeking inside one of the rooms.

"You'll see in a minute." He traces a hand over the side of

the bed. "I spent many summers here when I was younger," he says, thoughtful.

"I take it this was your room," I prod, taking a gander. If Connor had any belongings back then, they are clearly not here now. The bed takes up pretty much the whole room. There is nothing else in here besides a plain armoire. At the foot of the bed are the twin windows I saw when we came up to the house, the thick glass of the windowpane clouded with dust.

"Jessamine won't tell her neighbors who I am, will she?" I ask.

"My aunt is a very perceptive woman," he says, a playful glint in his eyes.

"A trait that runs in the family, I see."

"You can trust her," he adds. "Just don't expect her to treat you like a princess."

"Yet another trait that runs in the family," I tease.

He makes a sound that might be a laugh, and I can't help but chuckle in return.

"They've never lived under the rule of a monarch; they are not accustomed to our ways," he explains.

"You say that like it's a bad thing." I smile. "Believe me, I am more relieved than you know."

The way he looks at me stops my grin dead in its tracks, a look that makes me feel beautiful. The irony of it doesn't escape me, though, as I have never been so sullied. My hair, unkempt and frizzy, could not be more tangled. But just as I catch his gaze drift down to my lips, he clears his throat, dispelling the charged air between us.

"Let me show you to the bathhouse."

The faded green hem of Jessamine's dress falls long enough to drape the floor on me, the sleeves of the chemise stretching past my wrists, halfway to the tips of my fingers; I am glad there are no mirrors in the bathhouse. It's an open, wooden box with a door made of planks that swings outward on two rusty hinges. Inside, with my head and feet exposed for the world to see, there is a slab of wood to sit on, a large bucket of water, a cup from which to pour it, and a yellow bar of scentless soap.

Hair dripping wet, I stroll to the kitchen. The servants returning from the field throw curious glances in my direction. I pretend not to notice. I also resist the paranoid urge to cover my face. I tell myself that it is simple curiosity over a stranger, and not recognition. But growing up in a place where every single person knew who I am, it's a little hard to think otherwise. In the kitchen, Jessamine is busy throwing herbs into a large pot, giving an occasional stir with a wooden spoon. There is an elderly woman helping her, whom I presume is another servant, clad in a dress that appears to be made up of several layers of patched-up, cruddy fabrics. White strands of crimped hair jut out from her bonnet. When she notices me standing there by the doorway, she lifts her small nose at me with an air of hostility. I frown at her, not sure how else to respond to that, but she has already turned her back to me.

"Gertrude, this is my niece, Meredith," Jessamine says.

Niece? "Uh...hello," I say, stumbling over the word. Then it dawns on me that this must be an attempt to hide my identity and keep it from becoming gossip.

Gertrude merely acknowledges me with a grunt in my direction.

"Don't mind her; she's an old grouch," Jessamine says, shaking her fingers over the pot to sprinkle whatever she is holding.

Then a girl who looks about my age bursts into the kitchen, shoving me against the frame to get through.

"Where is he?" she demands, panting for breath.

"Hello to you to, Krea," Jessamine replies, not bothering to turn away from the pot.

When I hear Connor's steady footsteps coming down the stairs, Krea winds around, her red-haired braid swiveling with her. Fair skinned, full of freckles, she has green eyes that flick on me for a brief second, as if she is just now noticing my presence. I am about to greet her when she sprints past me. My eyes follow her down the short corridor, where I see Connor coming around the corner. Krea slams into him, throwing her arms around his neck. I watch as Connor's surprise melts into a smile and returns the hug. My stomach wrenches with displeasure. For a moment, it's all I can do but stand there, dumbfounded. But I realize I'm intruding on a private moment, so I turn my attention back to the ladies in the kitchen.

"Can I be of assistance?" I ask Jessamine. I have no expertise when it comes to cooking. However, I have baked a good number of pies. Well, no, I have helped Beth bake pies is more like it. Still, I think I did learn a thing or two.

Jessamine seems happy with my suggestion. "How nice of you to offer, dear," she says, gesturing for me to join her. Gertrude grunts.

Jessamine points me in the direction of a pile of fresh parsley. She hands me a knife and a small cutting board. "Chop those up for me, would you?"

"Yes madam," I answer. I can't deny that I am a bit excited to be doing kitchen work, even if it's something as simple as chopping herbs.

I don't get to do much chopping, however, because I happen to glance out the window and catch Connor and Krea walking around the dull garden. I'm not very successful at ignoring them either, as my eyes keep drifting back to the window. It's obvious that Krea, whoever she is, is ecstatic to see Connor again. I pretend to ignore the way she devours him with her eyes. There is a softness in Connor's manner that I have only recently witnessed when we greeted Jessamine, but for the most part, Connor seems impartial to her. Though to be fair, Connor is not the kind of man to wear his feelings on his sleeve.

I've chopped about a quarter of the bunch of parsley stems when I see Krea place a flirtatious hand on Connor's chest. A sharp, stinging pain shoots up from my index finger. I look down and gasp at the sight of blood. I stick my finger in my mouth, pressing the cut against my tongue, wincing at the surge of pain.

"What is it?" Jessamine asks, coming up beside me.

"Just a little cut," I say, though with my finger getting in the way of my tongue, it comes out sounding too muffled for her to understand.

With confusion wrinkled on the lines of her face, she looks over at the cutting board, where two drops of blood tell her what happened.

"Let me see that." She takes my finger from my mouth. With no pressure against it, blood flows out freely.

"You cut that finger good," she says, inspecting the gash. Then she simply presses my hand against the sleeve of my dress. "Keep your hand like that for a few minutes. Make sure you put enough pressure to stop the bleeding," she instructs.

"But the blood, won't it ruin your dress?"

She shrugs with one shoulder. "It's a very old dress dear, don't you worry. Now go have a seat in the parlor. Dinner will be ready in just a little while."

"What about the parsley?" I ask, glancing at my unfinished work.

"Gertrude will take care of it. Won't you, Gertrude?"

Gertrude responds with another grunt and I begin to wonder if she has a speech impediment.

I sit on a single chair by the unlit fireplace. I wait a good while before I unwrap my finger. A thin, deep cut traces across the width of the tip of my finger. It has stopped bleeding, but it still pulses with pain. A dark-red blotchy circle brands the sleeve, right above the crook of my elbow. This is what I get for being nosy. Who is that girl anyway? An old flame from his younger years? I stop myself. Connor is my escort. My protector. And maybe a friend. But that's all he ever will be. Because that is all he can be. But my resolve falters the moment Connor comes through the front door.

I sigh. I am in so much trouble.

"What happened?" Connor asks, his eyes on my arm as we sit down for dinner.

"I turns out parsley is not fond of being chopped," I mumble, mustering a weighty look.

I hear Krea snort from across the table.

Then Jessamine decides it's the perfect time to introduce us. "Meredith, this is Krea, my neighbor's daughter, a family friend. Krea this is my niece, Meredith."

Krea eyes me dubiously. "Your niece?"

Jessamine shoots her a warning look. "Yes. My niece. Gertrude will you please excuse us?"

Gertrude consents with yet another grunt. She leaves the dining room, but Jessamine remains quiet, glancing over her shoulder, as we all listen to Gertrude's steps fade away through the front door.

"Well, now that we have some food on the table," Jessamine says, gesturing at our steaming bowls of stew, "What in the Maker's name is going on?"

Connor doesn't hesitate to give them a rundown of the events leading up to our escape, so I can only assume that Krea is included in their circle of trust. He recounts everything in business-like fashion. The ghosts of terrifying moments flare in my mind with vivid detail.

Krea observes me from across the table, sizing me up, as though considering whether I'm worth all this trouble. Jessamine rubs her eyes, suddenly looking very tired. She extends a hand, clasping Connor's wrist. "You do what you need to get that girl to safety," she says, casting a pressing look.

"But don't get yourself killed," Krea adds, before dousing me with scorn.

"He's a survivor," Jessamine says proudly.

"He's not immortal, Jessamine," Krea counters.

Connor holds up his hands. "I'm sitting right here."

Krea roils with an exasperated sigh. "This isn't some petty enemy you're dealing with, Connor. Why are you taking such a risk?" she asks, briskly pointing her chin at me. "Why didn't you write to King Perceval? He can afford to send an army to retrieve her, can he not?"

"Rely on a messenger?" Connor questions in turn, eyebrows raised. "And then what? Wait a month or two, sitting like ducks? No. I couldn't take that risk."

"Yet you have no qualms about those men chasing after you?" she asks, folding her arms on the table.

Connor opens his mouth to speak but he seems to second-guess himself. In the end, he just exhales annoyance, pursing his lips.

To the relief of my empty stomach, Jessamine has the good sense to squash the debate. "Connor takes risks for a living, Krea, you know this. Maker knows we have enough problems around here to puzzle out. Let's eat our dinner before it gets cold."

And we all do. Except for Connor.

I have half the spoon in my mouth, tasting the savory broth of herbs and meat when he asks, "What problems?"

Jessamine draws up a napkin from her lap to wipe at the corners of her mouth. She clears her throat. "The same problems everyone else has around here," she says, exchanging a look with Krea.

Connor leans back in his chair. "Borderlords."

Jessamine and Krea nod grimly at Connor. The gesture sends a shiver down my arms.

"Those liver eaters think they have a right to keep increasing their fees," Jessamine shares with a scoff. "They know we can't afford it. But that is of no consequence to them; their greed is going to run us all into the ground."

"How are you managing the estate?" Connor asks.

"I had to let several workers go." A pained look pinches Jessamine's brow together with two small wrinkles. "Good working men, with families. But I will not let any more of them go. And I told them so. I set my foot down and gave those heathens a piece of my mind."

Connor leans on the table, eyes narrowed. "You refused to pay them?"

"I refused to pay them the difference."

Krea snaps her head at Jessamine, incredulity widening the whites of her pale green eyes. "How did they respond?" she asks.

Jessamine lifts her shoulders in a dismissive shrug. "They threatened me, said Zagar wouldn't be happy about it."

"Zagar?" I interrupt.

"He's the leader of the Borderlords," Connor explains.

"Aren't you worried of what they might do?" I ask Jessamine.

"Of course I am," she says, "But what choice do I have? I can't run this place if they keep raising their fees. Somebody has to put a stop to it.

"How long ago was it, when they came for payment?" Connor asks.

"Three days ago," Krea answers for her.

"I won't let them hurt you," Connor says, a protective, steely resolve ingrained in the set of his stare. Strangely, the sight of it makes me think of the other night at the inn, when he told me about his mother.

Jessamine affectionately pats Connor's hand. "Let's hope it doesn't come down to that."

Chapter Fifteen

Lying in bed, my thoughts whirl with dinner's conversation. I imagine a mob of angry men, armed with pitchforks and torches, making their way to the farm. I feel conflicted about Jessamine's actions. I support her reasoning; someone has to stop them. But it shouldn't have to be her. From all the stories I've heard, Borderlords are not to be trifled with. They have no governing body so they are free to do as they please. It's outrageous.

Krea is right to be angry. My ignorance is a common thing among the people of Stonefall. And by the looks of it, Alder doesn't care to dirty its hands with it, either. We've run from one problem only to plunge right into the middle of another.

I hear muffled steps on the stairs. Curious, I scoop myself

out of bed, throwing the sleeveless pajama coat that hangs on the wall over my nightdress. I open my door and tiptoe down the stairs like a shadow.

"Can't sleep either?" Connor asks as I glide off the last step. Settled by the window, he watches the hushed darkness that surrounds the house, like a hunter stalking for prey.

"I'm too tense for sleep," I say, easing up alongside him. "I'm worried about your aunt."

He nods. "This situation, it's not good. I brought you here, thinking it would be safe." He sighs, shaking his head. "I'm sorry."

It's subtle, but I see it. Strains of frustration line the sharp features of his face. The set of his eyes, furrowed skin in the space between them; jaw tight; lips pressed. He is torn between his duty to the king and that to his family.

I lay a reassuring hand on his shoulder, ignoring the saucy voice in my head that tells me I am simply using it as an excuse to touch him. "If we hadn't come, and something happened...Jessamine needs you here. She's family. And family is important, right? Besides, I feel much safer here than I did back home," I say, though the possibility of encountering the infamous Borderlords, and an unhappy lot at that, terrifies me to the core.

"We can't stay here forever," he mutters.

"Then let's help her however we can while we are here. And perhaps in Alder, we can do some good for the people of the Borderlands. Speak on their behalf. Inform King Perceval of what is happening here. Both kingdoms rely on these crops. Surely, he will take action against these injustices."

"He will," he says, confident. "It's the in between that worries me. My aunt is a strong woman; she knows how to defend herself. But she doesn't stand a chance against Zagar's men." Connor runs a flustered hand through his hair. "I wish she had asked for help before taking matters into her own hands."

I bite my lip, unsure of what to say. "What about the other farmers? Can we not rally them together to stand up against the Borderlords?"

"Perhaps," his says, studiously rubbing his chin. "I'm not sure that many would join; most people are too frightened to stand up for themselves."

"They might be willing if we give them the inspiration they need," I say, optimistic.

Connor glances at me. There's a smile in his eyes.

"What?" I ask, my stomach whisking with flutters.

"I think you have what it takes," he says.

I quirk an eyebrow. "To inspire them?"

"To be queen," he says in a quiet voice.

I feel my lips part with surprise. Charles's words come rushing back to me.

You will make a great queen one day.

I most certainly don't feel like a queen, or that I have what it takes, as he says. I am but an incompetent girl with good intentions.

"I appreciate the sentiment."

"No, you do. You just need some inspiration," he says, twisting his lips into a lopsided grin.

I try to imagine myself as queen. As a ruler. But even if he's right, even if I have what it takes to be queen, I would still only be a sapling, limited to the control of a king. How much difference could I really make? Then I remember what Connor said about the prince, that he's nothing like my father. Still, that knowledge fails to bring any real comfort. Because now, my wants and wishes have drifted, taking an unexpected turn, gravitating beyond the bounds of possibility.

Something in my face gives me away. "What is it?" Connor asks.

I wish I knew. "Oh, nothing."

Then, fidgeting with the stitching of my coat, I ask, "What will you do, once we make it to Alder?"

"That will be up to the king," he says, his watchful gaze back to the window.

Not satisfied with his answer, I press. "But you will be

around, won't you? We'll still see each other?"

"You won't need me at the castle. You'll be safe there."

That's what I'm afraid of. *Walk away*, warns the small voice in my head, almost inaudible.

But with a rebellious mind of its own, my body disregards everything. Pulse quickening, I reach for his hand, lacing my fingers around his.

"That's not it," I hear myself say.

Connor jerks his head around, looking down at our hands, and then at me. I see the unmistakable surprise, followed by a profound, incomprehensible haze, flaring from the remoteness of his thoughts. Then, in a heartbeat's flutter, he erases the marginal space between us, cupping my face in his hand.

And he kisses me.

While the world freezes in place, his lips press against mine, soft and demanding, and there is only him. All I hear is the hammering of my heart in my ears. All I feel is him. The kiss feels foreign and yet so natural. Instinctive. I give in without hesitation, drowning in the sensation of his lips on mine. I breathe him in, absorbing his dizzying, intoxicating scent. His free hand hooks around the small of my back, pulling me impossibly closer to him, and he deepens the kiss. But then he pulls away, taking a jagged step back. I almost lose my balance. It's strangely alluring to see him so alive. I watch him swallow and regain his composure.

"Forgive me," he says, his voice hoarse and unfamiliar.

Heart racing, my mind is still surging with a drunken desire when he briskly brushes past me, fading away up the stairs like a phantom.

And just like that, I am alone.

Chapter Sixteen

Sun hat secured around my chin, a sickle in hand, I follow Jessamine to the harvest field. An ocean of wheat ears stretches before us. The scattered line of farmers works at cutting the golden stems, their progress resting behind them, where others come to collect in baskets to take for deposit in the granaries. It's time-consuming labor, one that might prove arduous under the heat of the sun. But there are enough clouds sprinkled over the sky to create comfort.

We walk up to one of the farmers. "Why don't you help Emma collect the ears? We'll take it from here," Jessamine tells him. He nods his sweat-glossed head, handing his sickle to Jessamine.

She dives right in, requesting my observation. Her arms swing in a single motion, slicing a couple of handbreadths below the ears.

"Just like that," she says.

Alongside her, in the opposite direction, I mimic her instruction. Though clumsy, I find the task relatively easy. Once I get comfortable, it's not long before I find myself brooding over last night's kiss. It's been on my mind to the point of madness. All night I revisited the memory, fingers gingerly at my lips, awestruck, reliving every detail, every look, every touch. The whole thing feels surreal. As though I imagined it all. But no. It happened. It was real. Connor kissed me. And I kissed him back. The implications linger at the edges of my thoughts. But I can hardly think as it is.

I'm not sure what I would have said to him if I'd seen him this morning. He must have had the same dilemma, as he was absent at breakfast. He'd gone straight to help out in the field. But nervous as I am about it, avoiding him is the last thing I want to do. Which is partly why I'd been so eager to come out and work. But as luck would have it, I have yet to lay eyes on him.

"I have to admit, I'm surprised you volunteered to help," Jessamine says.

My guilty conscience burns at the corners of my cheekbones.

"Well, I couldn't just sit on my bum all day now, could I?"

She chuckles. "You might do just that after today's work."

I am not conditioned for hard labor, this is true. But I think I can make up for it in spirit. Just then, Krea comes calling from the direction of the house.

"Jessamine!"

She makes her way to us in long, confident strides. "I come with good news," she says through winded breaths. Then she catches sight of me under the hat.

"What is she doing here?" she asks through a raised brow.

"What does it look like I'm doing?" I snap, my eyes trailing to the sickle in my hands.

She regards me with a bemused purse of her lips, then turns her attention back to Jessamine. "My father and brothers have agreed to help you," she says, wearing a proud smile on her freckled face.

"Help me?" Jessamine asks.

"I told them what you did. They agree it's their duty as neighbors, and fellows of the trade, to assist you," she says.

Jessamine raises her chin slightly in a gesture of appraisal. "Thank you, Krea. But that is too much to ask of them; I risk my own neck because it's mine to risk."

Crossing her arms, Krea makes a stand. "Really? You don't seem to have a problem risking Connor's neck."

Anger tightens in Jessamine's brow. "If you think I don't concern myself with my nephew's life, you are gravely mistaken. But I don't make his decisions for him. And there's no amount of dissuading that would make him change his mind. Now, you listen to me. I understand you care a great deal about him, but I will not tolerate this brazenness of yours, is that clear?"

Krea evades the question. "Then my family's decision to help is theirs to make, not yours," she argues with an air of finality, turning her back to us and marching away.

Unlike me, Jessamine doesn't waste a second watching her go. She simply returns to the task at hand as though nothing happened. I follow suit, but can only go so long without asking the question eating at my tongue.

"Krea and Connor...are they...?" I struggle with the question, tangled in my mouth.

Jessamine sighs, wistful. "That poor girl has been infatuated with Connor since she was little. She always used to say she was going to marry him one day. They would have made a fine match, those two. Perhaps he would have taken an interest in her, if only he hadn't lost his mother. Everything changed after that. We were all affected by it, but it hit him the hardest. He would scarcely speak; there were days when he did not cast out a single word. He would just sit silently, a faraway look on his face, tracing that scar of his. My brother brought him to me, hoping it would do him some good to be elsewhere. For a while we thought he would never snap out of it. He did, eventually, but he was never the same boy again."

Connor's aloofness, his cool reserve, it all makes sense to me now. Watching his mother die scarred him in more ways than one. It hardened him. "I'm sorry."

"It was a long time ago," she says.

Several blisters later, the work is deemed done for the day. After a hard days' work, a quarter of the wheat has been cut. The workers look drained, constantly wiping at their brows. But their bodies carry them along, accustomed to the monotonous strain. I, on the other hand, move along about as fast as a caterpillar. Jessamine is eager to get dinner prepped. She makes haste through the field, blending among the servants. I don't try to keep up. The sickle seems to have gained a pound or two. It felt light in my hands this morning. Now it feels heavy and cumbersome. My blistered hand is numb, and I lose my sloppy grip on the sickle. It thumps flatly on the ground.

I stretch a wary hand to pick it up, groaning from the strain in my back as I bend down to reach it, when another hand beats me to it.

"Oh. Hello," I mutter. Just the sight of Connor brings a flushed heat to my face. My arms and hands have all but forgotten how spent they are. But there is nothing welcoming in his features. Nothing to hint that we shared something last night. Nothing to suggest he kissed me. I am reminded of the hawk-eyed stranger who saved me from a violent drunkard. The stranger whose gaze had yet to soften. The stranger who had yet to smile at me. Sharp, tiny needles prickle at my heart. The silly giddiness; the excited nervousness; the thrilling wonder— it is all instantly squashed.

Looking past me, he moves on. Crushed, I stare at his back, unsure if I should say something. I want to say something. Anything. But words escape me. I am at a loss.

Noticing I am not following behind, he stops to look at me. For a fleeting moment, I think I catch a trace of what I'd seen in him last night.

"You coming?" he asks.

After two full days of harvesting wheat, my hands are raw and worn. On the palm, just below where the fingers connect with the hand, raised, reddened bumps feel rough to the touch, estranged from the ivory smoothness around them. What of the heart, though? Does it also have the power to grow a layer of thick skin? Connor and I haven't spoken. As if it never happened. He doesn't avoid me; he has been present for breakfast and dinner, and he continues to sit next to me at the table, but he does not speak to me. I dare say he doesn't even glance my way.

Because try as I might, I can't avoid stealing guarded looks at him, hoping to meet his eye. In the flutter of a bird's wing, I've become the hairline crack in the wood, present yet easily overlooked; absorbed into the background. I prompt myself to remember that this is for the best. But somewhere in the deepest, darkest corners of my heart, this truth is not accepted. I must figure out a way to speak to him in private. It turns out today is my lucky day.

"You are not going out to the field today," Jessamine informs me as I secure the sun hat atop my head.

"May I ask why?" I say.

"You have worked hard the past few days, but you are not seasoned for labor like the rest of us. You must rest."

As pleasing as it sounds to get a break, spending hours alone with nothing to do but wallow in my thoughts is probably not the best idea.

"I rested plenty last night."

Her eyebrows rise skeptically, emphasizing the lines across her forehead. "You expect me to believe that with those dark circles under your eyes?"

I don't need a mirror to confirm it. Sleep has been hard to come by. "I feel fine. I can handle it."

She grabs at my hands, turning them over to show the swollen palms. "Definitely not," she commands.

I breathe a defeated sigh. "Is there something else I could do?"

She lifts her forefinger and thumb to frame her sun-weathered face. "Well, if you must, I suppose you could see if Connor needs help with the fence. I doubt he does, but he might enjoy the company," she says with a smile.

I choke on a bitter laugh and nod.

On this particular morning, the clouds are not present to shield us from the sweltering sun. I'm glad I decided to keep the hat on. The expanse of the field blurs in hazy heat waves of gold and brown. Beyond it, the fence stands like a dotted line in the distance. The closer I get, the faster my heart pounds. And when my eyes discern Connor's kneeling silhouette, it gives way to walloping thumps, skittish and agitated.

Ruffling through waist-high wheat stalks, I'm sure he hears me coming from yards away. Halting his busy hands, he locks on to my approach, and for a moment, he just watches me. Unwavering. But he turns back to his work before I get close enough to make out his countenance.

"What are you doing here?" he asks, keeping busy with the hammer he drives into the wood.

"Jessamine asked me to come help you." I intended to speak confidently, but instead I sound like a cornered mouse.

"I don't need help."

"Yes, I see that."

As the silence ensues, I can almost hear his back asking why I'm still here. But as uncomfortable as I feel, I'm not about to let him brush me off so easily.

"What happened to the fence?" I ask. I think I hear him groan under his breath.

"It's old wood. Brittle," is all he says.

"So you're replacing it with new wood?"

"Yes."

"And you have all you need? You don't need me to fetch anything for you?" I ask, my hands studiously tangled at my back.

He wipes his brow. "Yes. And no."

Irritation builds in my chest. Why does he insist on punishing me? He kissed me, after all. Just how many nerves must I pinch for him to speak his mind?

"I'll just keep you company then," I say casually.

"No need. I'm almost finished."

"Oh. We can walk back together then," I quip. *Let's see you wiggle yourself out of this one.*

While he joists a new wooden post, I quietly garner the courage to assert myself. *We need to talk.* No. That gives him ample opportunity to brush it off. *About the other night...*better. In the end, I opt for a more direct approach.

"Why did you kiss me?" I utter the words in haste, afraid that

I might bite them back before they are spoken.

At once Connor stops hammering. His shoulders sag, but he doesn't face me. "It was a mistake," he says finally, in a low, dissonant voice.

A brief, sharp pain grazes my insides, leaving a strange, out of place feeling in its wake. My hands ball up into tight, clenching fists. "Then why did you do it?" I ask.

He turns, his blue eyes on fire, but he does not answer my question. He just stares. I ask again. "*Why?*"

"Because I love you," he says.

The words are so staggering that it takes several whooshing heartbeats for their meaning to sink in.

He loves me.

My heart soars. But then it plummets. "How can you say that when you avoid me like I'm a walking plague?"

A keen disquiet settles in his gaze. "You are not mine to love."

I draw back. This is a view I have never been able to come to terms with. "I belong to no one."

He shakes his head. "We are bound by our duty," he clarifies.

Bound by duty. I have grown up with that reality rooted into my soul. Yet here I am, nearly willing to ignore it. All because of him. And here he is, claiming that he loves me as he pushes me away.

"I know that," I say, hating the palpable disappointment in my voice.

He swallows, slow and hesitant. "Meredith...any feelings you may have for me, you need to rid yourself of them. As will I. We'll put this behind us and never speak of it again. Agreed?"

Rid myself of my feelings? Is that even possible? And what is it that I feel, exactly? What is he asking me to bury to the depths of oblivion? Do I love him? I don't know.

With a lump in my throat, I muster the word. "Agreed."

Chapter Seventeen

A sheen of gray light filters through the windows. I am happy, relaxed, weightless, like a dandelion floating in the breeze. Beth is here. She smiles at me, holding up a tray of bread, straight out of the oven. The bread is burned. A bitter smell singes my nostrils. And the serenity that surrounds me ebbs away, leaving me with a subdued sense of awareness, conscious of a reality that isn't there. I hear something. Faintly. Like the buzzing of a gnat at my ears. I focus. *Wake up*.

Sunlight is fading. "Beth?" I ask, reaching out to my friend, who seems to be disappearing into the darkness.

"Wake up!"

Connor grips me by the shoulders, his eyes urgent. The fog

of sleep tapers off. The Borderlands. The farm. It's the middle of the night. Connor is fully dressed; armed. I dart up to my elbows. Then I smell it. Smoke.

My eyes widen as fear surges like a storm into my chest. "Is the house burning?"

He shakes his head. "The harvest. I need you to stay here. Do not come out unless it's me or Jessamine coming to check on you."

"What? No," I protest with a frown. "I want to help." I move to get up but he holds me back, a gentle yet firm palm against my breastbone.

"If Borderlords are behind this, I don't want you out there."

The farm can't survive without the wheat. A whole season's worth of hard labor, undone in the blink of an eye.

"All right," I reluctantly mutter under my breath.

Connor is already on the move.

"Be careful," I say. Does he hear the weight of my words? The underlying fear in them?

If he does, he makes no sign of it. He gives me a short nod before dashing out the door, swinging it shut to enclose me in the shelter of the room.

When the house falls silent, I edge to the window, knowing I won't be able to get a glimpse of anything. The field lies behind the house. From here, I can only observe hints of the fire, an orange-pink glow that intermingles with the indigo blue of the night sky. And here I am doing nothing while the wheat, and surely the granaries, burn. All that work. But Maker forbid the fragile princess join the cause and burn a finger. Connor is right, though. If those men are out there, the best way I can help is by steering clear of them.

Hands and head stagnant on the glass, there is only my own, drawn out breaths, fogging the dust sprinkled glass. That's when I hear it. A distant shatter. I hear another. And another.

What in the Maker's gate...?

My hand hesitates at the doorknob. *Do not come out,* Connor orders in my head, but the mayhem continues. I draw my fingers back an inch. But the smashing and splintering does not relent. It picks up in roaring waves, with only brief respites in between. And I can't take it anymore.

Peering over the landing, I see the parlor is in shambles. The wooden floorboards are littered with broken items. The fireplace looks barren. All the trinkets and candlesticks that adorned it have been tossed among the clutter. There is another burst of sound, a booming clatter of metal. I give a start, skittering backwards. The floor creaks, and the restless rifling below dies down abruptly.

Stupid, stupid, stupid!

Hearing someone approaching, I scurry back to my room. I

slam my weight against the door. I don't need to look around for options or ideas, because there are none. I either hide or jump out the second-story window. I hurl all my strength against the door, hoping he's some weakling that can't overpower me.

The footsteps advance up the stairs in a flurry, but as they make it to the hallway they slow to a cautious tread. I hold deathly still, my arms and legs stiff from the effort. I don't even dare let out a breath. Outside my door is a Borderlord. I know it. A cool, clammy layer of sweat spreads across my face. If he doesn't choose this door, then maybe, just maybe, it will give me enough of a head start to run out to the field.

And then the door gives way underneath my palms, opening just a crack, but the pressure of my weight forces it back. He rams the door, and this time it opens enough for him to stick his arm through it. A hand with blackened fingernails swipes at my arm, clutching a handful of my sleeve. Panic gives me a boost of strength, and I levy it on the door, shoving it back until it pinches his arm. With a low growl, he pulls it free, and the door slams closed with a bang.

Without reprieve, I brace myself for the next blow, exerting all the energy I can muster to keep the door closed. My hands swell from the effort. I can't keep this up. I feel the stamina drain out through my pores with each second that passes. The Borderlord bashes the door with a brute strength that sends me sprawling. Reeling backward, I lose my balance, crashing to the floor as the Borderlord barges in. The first thing I notice is the beastly tattoo on his face. A perfectly inked eye covers the whole of his right cheek. Snakes crawl around it in a wreath of entwined scales. Another tattoo, one of a snake, slithers across the bridge of his nose to his other cheek.

The Borderlord smiles, revealing a severe lack of teeth.

"Well, well, well. What have we here?" he says, sounding all too pleased with himself. "Where did you come from, little morsel?"

I grit my teeth, answering with a muted glare.

"The missus hid you well, but it's a good thing I found ya. She has a debt to pay, you see."

I inch away, my eyes darting nervously between him and the open door.

He takes a step closer, offering me his hand. "I won't hurt you, if you come willing."

I get up, slowly, my eyes cautiously fixed on him, and then on his hand. In a passive motion, I extend my arm out to let him take hold. He clamps his dirty fingers around my wrist, a satisfied grin on his lips.

He pulls me close. "That's a good gir—"

I hike my knee up, thrusting into his groin. The Borderlord doubles over, groaning. Shoving him hard onto the floor, I take off like a gazelle. Dashing down the stairs, I hear him shuffle back to his feet. As I run across the foyer, over the chaos of broken objects, I feel the sharp bite of broken glass pierce into my bare foot. I stop, scooping my foot up in my hand. A thick, jagged piece of glass protrudes from the ball of my foot. I yank the shard out. Blood oozes, but I don't have time to press against the wound.

The Borderlord growls after me, crushing his way down the stairs as I stagger out the front door on one foot. There's no telling what he'll do if he catches me. *When he catches me.* Limping away, it's only a matter of time before he does. I have to run. But the moment I put my foot down on the gravel, a wave of serrated pain shoots up my leg, and my resolve falters. When the Borderlord storms out after me, I urge myself to try again. Pain burns the sole of my foot. Tears prick my eyes as I will my legs to keep moving. Coming around the garden, I see it—the fire. Surging flames light up the dark sky, tainting its clarity with billowing clouds of smoke. And there are people. Lots of them. Their shadows hurry through the field of fire with buckets of water. If only I could reach them, but they are so far away.

The Borderlord tackles me. My cheek smashes against the dirt. Small rocks dig into my skin. Tangled under his crippling weight, I resort to the most basic of instincts.

I scream.

Chapter Eighteen

The screeching cry for help explodes in my chest. It tears through my throat with a life of its own. The Borderlord turns me over to face him and a fist comes crashing down on my cheekbone. I feel the force of the blow split my skin open. He drags me to my feet, his hand forcefully pinning my arms behind me.

He presses a sharp, pointed object at my neck. "You try that again and I will slit your throat," he warns in my ear. The rancid bitterness of his breath stirs disgust in my stomach.

In a daze, I let him yank me away, ignoring the pain that springs with every other step I take. He tugs me back, past the garden and the house, into the empty darkness of the road, until finally he stops. At once, I lift my foot up and hold it, just above the ground. The pulsating pain subsides a little, and I allow myself a soft sigh of relief. I look over my shoulder. The Borderlord works at untying a horse from a fence post with one hand, while the other clutches my wrists together. I can feel my fingers start to go numb.

He's taking me back to the Borderlords. To their camp. And I don't dare wonder for what. I could jerk free of his hold. I know I could. His grip is tight, but it's only one hand. But his warning holds me in place, because with an injured foot, I won't get very far, and he will catch me again. And he will kill me. The helplessness that pounds in my chest is maddening. Wounded, beaten, and afraid, I am payment for a debt.

Looking up in the direction of the house, I see movement. Just a distant trace of it, cutting through the canvas, like a rustle of leaves in a field of grass. My confidence returns like a bolt of lightning. It's him. I know it. I feel it in the sudden rush of blood that pumps me back to life. It takes all that's left of me not to scream his name. Having freed his horse, the Borderlord stands behind me to lift me up on the saddle. As he does, I slam my head backward into his skull. Somehow, the pain does not bother me. In fact, I welcome it. The Borderlord drops me, stumbling and cursing. I move as fast as the open wound on my foot allows, which is faster than I thought possible. But not fast enough. With every step I take, the snarls and hasty breaths get closer and closer, and I don't have to look back to know that he will be on me in a matter of seconds.

Connor won't get to me in time. The man will slit my throat. I hear Connor's faint, swift command.

"Down!"

I throw myself on the empty road, skidding across it from the momentum, scraping my hands and knees against dirt and rocks as I roll to a stop.

Heart pounding, I flip over to brace against a strike, or the cut of a blade. But what I see is a blur, a confident whoosh of air that glides in the blink of an eye. Two strides away, the Border-lord stares but not at me. He paws at his chest, pierced by what is suddenly a most comforting sight. An arrow. Relief spreads in my trembling limbs. The Borderlord falls like an empty shell. I sit there, unable to peel my eyes away. For a moment, just a brief moment, I think of the jousting contestant from long ago, who fell off his horse, fatally wounded by the blunt blow of the lance. How different I had looked upon that death. As for the man who lies before me, dead and bleeding, I revel in his death, satisfied in a vindictive way. A part of me recoils at this Meredith, appalled at my own spite. But for some reason, I can't bring myself to look away.

It's not until Connor kneels before me that the invisible link breaks. I gratefully take in his ash-smeared face. Through ragged breaths, his sharp eyes inspect my wounds, trailing from the rawness of my cheek to my foot. He appears to be unscathed. No signs of burns or injury. *Thanks be to the Maker*, I pray wordlessly.

Then, without a word, he gently takes me in his arms. He holds me, silent and tender. And I feel as though I could cry forever on his shoulder. But I don't. Somehow, I hold it in. I keep that brittle sheet of glass from cracking. My trembling hands come up to the nape of his neck and pull him against me.

Safe. I'm safe.

Despair hovers over us like a storm cloud as we take in the gutted house. Jessamine, Krea, Gertrude, three male servants, Connor, and myself. We are all that remains. What used to be the parlor is now a wrecked, unrecognizable space, with an empty table standing in the midst of the clutter. The mess is overwhelming. It will take some time to sift through the broken, irreparable goods and ornaments to find whatever may be worth salvaging. But at least the second floor remains intact.

Connor carried me back to the field, where servants and neighbor farmers alike concentrated their efforts to extinguish the last of the fire. My heart sank at the sight of the destruction, more than half of the wheat field scorched black. The Borderlords had sent a single man to do the job.

"They want to make an example out of me," Jessamine deduces, breaking the glum silence. She looks at no one, her eyes downcast on the table, where she rests her weight on clenched fists. "This farm is my life. And they have crippled me, but I will mend my wounds. I will rise again." Her dignified gaze falls on the three servants. Her eyes shine with tears that do not spill. "You tell the others I will restore this farm," she commands, her voice breaking. Her grief pains me, and guilt creeps at the corners of my mind, because she is in need of consolation, and it should be Connor who comforts her, yet he does not leave my side. I look up at him now, my eyes questioning him. He meets my gaze, giving a slight shake of his head. *Is she too proud?* I wonder.

The servants obediently nod, though uncertainty lingers in their spent, blackened faces.

"We will help you rebuild," Krea says, looking to Connor for affirmation.

"No," Jessamine says flatly. "I need Connor's help elsewhere."

"Elsewhere?" Krea echoes, suddenly alert.

Jessamine directs herself to Connor. "The Borderlords give me no choice but to succumb to their demands. I need you to speak on my behalf to King Perceval."

"Of course. But you must come with me. I can't leave you behind, not after this," he says, gesturing at the room.

"They have already punished me. I need only give them what they ask for and they will let me be," Jessamine says with assurance.

"And what of their dead man? You think they are going to let you get away with that?" Connor asks.

Jessamine's expression stirs with rage and helplessness. "I will not leave this farm. You can't ask me to do that. This place is my life, your uncle's legacy. I will not do it!"

Connor lets out a vexed breath. "Aunt," he starts, but Jessamine cuts him off.

"No," she says sharply, lifting a warning finger at him. They exchange a heated glance before she storms up the stairs.

In the stunned silence that follows, Gertrude and the servants slowly and uncomfortably make their way out the front door.

"Will the king do something about this?" I ask Connor.

His solemn eyes linger on the stairs. "He will."

"He won't," Krea sneers. "They are all too preoccupied selecting a menu for their next banquet. They don't care about us. Out of sight, out of mind, isn't that right, Connor?" She utters the last words like a fist to the face.

Connor replies with measured words. "No. It isn't."

Krea hikes her eyebrows. "Oh? Well, by all means then. Go.

Speak to your gracious king. But don't worry, we won't hold our breath," she says, shoving past us with disdain.

"She seems a bit more ruffled than usual," I observe. *Maybe you should go talk to her*, I almost add, but the thought of him chasing after her brings a sour taste to my mouth.

"She'll settle down. Come, let's get that foot cleaned." He hunkers down to lift me up in his arms, and I fail miserably to escape from my own feelings.

Outside, the night air is dry with the acrid stench of smoke, overpowering even now, as though the flames were burning still. It clings to our skin, our hair, our garments. Connor lays me down on the slab inside the bathhouse, drawing a bucket from the well.

"You don't have to do this," I say, watching him, but my suggestion falls on deaf ears.

On his knees, he cleanses his hands, and then carefully scoops up my injured foot, rinsing and soothing the wound.

"This will sting," he warns, as he reaches for the soap. I stiffen as it makes contact with the raw flesh. It stings all right, like stepping on needles. But once he rinses the soap, the pain subsides instantly, as if it was never there to begin with.

"Thank you," I say quietly. "Not just for this but for back there, on the road. You saved my life." He lifts his head, finding my gaze. He peers at me with thinly veiled longing. The space inside my ribcage swells with a warm, fuzzy feeling.

"I shouldn't have left you behind," he says, echoing with self-loathing. "I should have known."

"You couldn't have known. None of us did." My hands itch to reach out to him.

"For a second there I thought I was too late. I haven't felt fear like that since..." He doesn't say it, but he doesn't have to. In the darkness, his eyes seem bright, stirring with feelings I know he will not express, feelings he promised to forget. But then I watch him struggle with himself, seeming vulnerable. Exposed.

I slip off the slab to kneel before him, neglecting the dull pain that reminds me of my scraped knees. I gently trace his scar with the tip of my index finger. Raised and smooth, I feel the emotion behind it. The heartache it embodies.

"Meredith..." he trails off.

"Tell me," I plead softly.

His voice strains to a whisper. "I lied to you...when I said I would forget. I don't think I can. Not ever." he takes my hands, his thumbs stroking my open palms. "I am not the sort of man who falls in love. Yet here I am, hopelessly in love with you."

The smoky air around me seems to thicken. If this is his idea of burying our feelings, well, it's not working.

But he isn't finished. "This"—he holds my hand up to his

chest, his heart—"is permanent. There is no amount of denying that will make it go away."

And there it is.

I kiss him.

With a groan, he pulls me close. Though his hands press against my back, yearning and wanting, he kisses me slowly, gently, as though kissing me is the only thing that makes sense.

He draws back, breathing hard. There is candor and zeal in his eyes, an outspoken gaze. Then, seemingly unable to help himself, his lips fall back into mine. We kiss, again and again. Insatiable. Two young lovers, defying the world. Defying destiny. *Destiny*. The word cuts like a knife, because I know that Connor is not written in my stars.

We are bound by duty.

This time it's me who draws back. Now that I can regain my wits, or a part of them, I notice the drumming of his heart beneath my hands. He peers at me through half-lidded eyes, and I feel as though I could melt in his arms. But I force myself to focus.

"Please tell me you have a plan," I whisper.

"Not exactly," he says with a sigh, resting his temple atop my head.

"How will I ever live with myself if...if I...my people." *If I allow Theros to dominate and slaughter my people.* The awful words get stuck in my throat. It's so selfish. I can't bring myself to speak them.

He pulls away to look me in the eye. "I would never ask that of you," he says solemnly.

A small candlelit hope flares in me, flickering and wavering. "Are you saying there's another way?"

"Are you sure this is what you want?" he asks, his eyes probing and hopeful.

For a moment, I almost laugh. Is it what I want? As if it isn't the most obvious truth in the world. I've never been more certain about anything as I am about him. But seeing the expectant gravity with which he awaits an answer, I realize that my wants and desires are not as clear to him as they are to me.

"I am sure," I say, a warm smile tugging at the corners of my mouth.

His eyes brighten and he smiles, a full-fledged, ear-to-ear, heart-stopping smile. "Then I will find a way."

Chapter Nineteen

After what happened last night at the bathhouse, nothing is capable of damping my spirits. Luckily, none of the servants seem to notice. They are quite preoccupied with sifting through the broken hopes of the house. As I should be. By the time I woke up, Connor had already left to take care of any loose ends from the confrontation with the Borderlord. Jessamine left early, too, bound for the field, refusing to mope and determined to get her farm back on track. She licked her wounds and rolled up her sleeves, ready to take on the challenge. I couldn't help but admire her, envious, in a good sort of way, of her strength.

Krea storms in the front door. I never thought it would be possible for her pale face to lack more color, but I stand corrected. She looks ghastly.

"Get your things," she orders, looking at me.

"I don't—I didn't bring anything with me," I stammer.

She rolls her eyes. "Get your princess bottom moving then!"

I lift my brow at her. "And just where am I supposed to move my bottom to?"

"Follow me."

She leads me through the field, past the charred remains and what is left of the harvest, away from Jessamine and her workers. She glides quickly, but I can't keep up with her; my foot still hurts when I put weight on it so I have to settle for a hurried limp.

"Krea? *Where* are we going?" I ask, flustered. I can't believe I am actually trailing after her, like some lost puppy. If it weren't for the fear I'd seen in her eyes, I probably wouldn't have.

She doesn't answer. I hasten my stride, groaning at the pain as I trot up to her. I clutch at the end of her waist-long braid, and with a swift tug, I pull her to a stop.

"Ow!" she cries out, scratching at the base of her skull. Her usual fierceness returns in full force, all trace of fear absent, and she directs it at me.

"You asked for it," I blurt out, before she can curse the living daylights out of me. "I will not take another step until you tell me what is going on."

The whites of her eyes flare with rebellion. "We don't have time for this," she barks. And then proceeds to clasp a hand around my wrist.

My free hand comes up, balled into an angry fist, landing smack against her freckled nose. The impact sends a pang through my knuckles. I see blood smeared along the fingers she holds up to her nose.

I raise a hand to my mouth. "Oh, Maker. I am so sorry."

She regards me with surprise and curiosity. "Not bad, princess. I didn't think you had it in you."

"I didn't break your nose, did I?" I ask, contrite.

She shakes her head, slumping her shoulders with a sigh. "Borderlords are questioning my family at this very moment," she says, wiping at her nose. "They are searching for their missing member, and they believe my brothers are involved. Connor and I hid the body this morning, but given that they already presume him dead, it hardly makes a difference. There is no telling what they will do. But Connor can't get involved; it will only escalate things. And he is our only chance at ending all of this."

My thoughts turn to Jessamine and I fill with dread. What will they do to her now? "I thought you were opposed to speaking to the king?"

"I was. I am still. But the others have hope," she says with a shrug. "Either way, I prefer it if Connor leaves now, before something happens to him. Now, will you please just come with me? He will meet up with us."

At a neighboring field, Connor awaits our arrival by Diago's side under the shade of a lonesome sycamore tree. Even at a distance, I can see him pacing, arms at his waist. Uneasy. But the pacing tapers off the instant his head turns in our direction.

"Here she is, just as I promised," Krea says through a smirk.

"Thank you," he says, giving her a curt nod. "Your brothers are safe, for now."

"They found the trail then?" Krea asks, sounding pleased.

"The trail?" I interrupt, too curious to keep quiet.

"Connor used that bootlicker's horse to leave a misleading trail." Krea makes a playful walking motion with her index and middle finger. "It should keep them busy for a while."

"And what happens when they turn their attention back to your brothers? To Jessamine?" I ask.

"Leave that to us. You've got bigger problems," Krea says.

"We should go," Connor pipes in, hinted with a sense of urgency.

Krea moves to put her arms around Connor. Her embrace, hard and strong, voices the unspoken concern. "Make haste."

Chapter Twenty

We cross the border into Alder three days later. A dreamlike feeling settles over me. The border town of Far Water, glowing as the sun sinks on the horizon, is the first indication we've passed onto Alderian soil. But even out here in the countryside, signs of the kingdom's robust economy are clear. Shops of square rubble masonry populate the cobbled town, with quaint signs of rich wood dangling before their doors. The cozy streets diverge from a tasteful town square where flower merchants roam. It is a merchant town. And even though it is just as busy as one would expect, it's peaceful, too. Guards patrol the confined streets in pairs, clad in chainmail, metal arm guards and greaves, with the gold lion crest prominently displayed over their blue uniforms.

They keep a watchful eye, though their numbers are scant. No doubt, King Perceval saves the legion for where they are needed most.

At the inn, tucked away from everyone and everything, I ease into Connor's arms, which gladly gather me up into him. With my head against his chest, I inhale the surreal newness of him. Of us. Impossible and true. Unexpected and immutable. Awry and perfect.

"How much farther to Alder Castle?" I ask. I don't want to stop, not even for our much-needed rest. *Make haste.* And yet, I dread the destiny that awaits me there.

"A fortnight," he murmurs, kissing the top of my head.

Two weeks. A whole month will easily rush by before help arrives at the Borderlands. Will that be soon enough for Jessamine? Or too late? Judging by Connor's pained gaze, he must be wondering the same thing.

"We should keep going," I mutter.

"No. We've hardly stopped. Even if we could manage, Diago needs rest."

A bleak smile turns my lips. "I can't say no to that."

"We'll leave at dawn," he says, cupping my chin. His eyes search for signs of agreement.

"All right, fair enough," I concede, and cringe at the glee that surges in my heart, as though we could delay arriving altogether.

But then I recall Connor's words that night at the bathhouse. He said he'd find a way. But I can't truly believe there is one.

"Connor..." I begin, hesitant. "You have a plan, right?"

The flicker of doubt that crosses his face floods me with unease. He takes in a breath, his chest slowly expanding and then compressing as he exhales. "I will ask King Perceval for his blessing and approval."

My breath catches in my throat. Has he lost his mind? I find myself unable to reconcile his words. Maker, he could very well get himself beheaded for such outlandish behavior.

"You cannot be serious," I manage to say, stricken with incredulity.

To my surprise, he almost smiles. That coveted curve of his lips teases me, there and gone in a heartbeat. "I'm afraid jest is not one of my talents."

I crinkle my brow, wanting to both laugh and throw a fist at that boldly handsome face of his. "It's not funny," I grumble.

"Do you trust me?" he asks, stroking my cheek with the back of his hand.

The answer bellows in my mind, deep-rooted in my every fiber. I trust him. With my life. With my heart. With everything.

"Yes," I whisper finally.

He draws me up in a kiss. A calm, gratified kiss. When he pulls away, he says, "You will understand when we get there."

This only leaves me more stumped than I was to begin with. But I don't press, satisfied that I will understand soon enough.

And with that thought locked away, another takes its place.

Sleeping arrangements.

The empty bed might as well be a blaring sign that reads: *Mate*. He doesn't expect...does he? The short hours of sleep we've had since we left the farm have been spent entwined in each other's arms. Ironically though, thoughts of intimacy never once crossed my mind. But here, the reality of it is about as easy to ignore as a waving red flag. My mouth starts to runs dry and I feel my muscles tighten. Still holding me close, Connor notices the change.

"Is something wrong?" he asks.

I swallow, hoping to rid myself of the aridness at the back of my tongue. It's probably best if I just say it, get it out of the way. Direct and to the point.

"Um...," I mumble, my gaze trailing to the neatly folded, embroidered covers of the bed.

I tried.

But in good time, Connor's perceptiveness spares me the mortification. "I'll sleep on the floor," he says. And yet, relieved as I am, sleeping apart from him seems nonsensical. Unbearable.

"No, don't," I softly object. "I'll just end up on the floor my-self." I joke, though it is hardly a lie. I probably would crawl to his side in the middle of the night, searching the dark for the comfort of his arms.

He gladly obliges. And as the quiet town of Far Water draws its shutters closed, I bury myself in the scent of leaves and soil and steady breaths, and let the transparent happiness that glows in my chest sweep me off to sleep.

Before sunrise, Connor and I ready ourselves for another long journey. Ripping a strip of fabric from the hem of my skirt, I gather my hair up into a braid. As for nourishment and provisions, we are better prepared this time. With pecans, sun-dried salted meat, and two leather canteens filled to the brim with Far Water wine, I feel fit for travel. Out on the indigo-lit street, welcoming fire light dances through several shop windows as the owners inside prepare for another day.

By the time we leave the stables, the sun is already rising in the east, lighting the violet sky anew with a layer of rosy pink. As we progress further, the streets widen, and the number of houses and shops dwindle to just a few, slowly replaced by stretches of picturesque vineyards and empty fields. Diago moves at a casual gait, content to be rested and fully fed. The law that prohibits riders to hasten their horses until they are entirely out of town has always appealed to my sensibility; it was established and adopted by both Alder and Stonefall in the years of the treaties, to prevent accidental deaths by trampling.

My arms circle comfortably around Connor's waist. He laces a hand through mine, while the other holds on to the reins. I am just resting my chin on his shoulder when my eyes focus on the blur of a horse, tied up outside what looks to be a small cottage. In itself, the sight is nothing of interest. Except the horse picks at my brain for some odd reason. Then I realize it's the horse's coat that warrants my undivided attention, a familiar shade of cara-mel. But no, it can't be Daisy. My heart beats with melancholy at the memory of her. I miss her, so naturally, my eyes see what they want to see. But as we near the cottage, the horse picks up Diago's steady approach and raises its head to look at us. *Daisy?* My head tallies its memories of her, riding lessons, brushing her shiny mane, feeding her stolen pieces of fruit from the kitchen. All the memories lead me to one that is fresh and vivid: the night at the stables; watching her leave with a friend.

Holt. And James.

Where did they say they were going? I flick my gaze to the cottage. A vegetable garden, only a few yards in diameter, lies behind it. A short wooden fence wraps around it. Compared to the lavish green land around it, the cottage stands out. With eve-ry second that passes, my eyes discern more and more of the an-imal.

Daisy. It *is* her.

A grin takes over my lips, pushing them to the corners of my face. I was certain I'd never come upon her again. But incredibly, there she is. As her stare lingers, I realize she must also recognize me.

"Stop!" I say to Connor, exuberant.

In a blink, Connor pulls on the reins.

Before he can ask, I am jumping off the horse. I land gracelessly on hands and feet. Connor calls after me, concerned, as I run up to Daisy. I throw my arms around her neck.

"Oh, I've missed you so," I say, holding on tight.

When I draw back to pet her nozzle, Connor joins me. "I take it this is your horse?" he asks, though he says it more like a statement than a question.

"Daisy," I say with an overjoyed nod. I can practically feel my face beaming. "I sent her away with James and Holt; the night I helped them escape."

He lays a hand at her side. "She's beautiful."

And well behaved, I muse, releasing the knot that ties her to the porch. They clearly don't know my horse as well as I do. She wouldn't wander off, not far anyway. Daisy nudges against my face, letting me know she is happy to see me.

"Meredith? Is that you?"

I wheel around to meet a familiar face. Holt stands just off the side of the cottage, donning a pair of dirty gardening gloves and a hat. The tentative smile on his face builds to a wide, toothy grin. I laugh, too excited to think straight, and make a beeline for him, locking him in a bear hug.

"Maker." He shakes his head in disbelief. "What are you doing here?"

I gesture at Connor, who waits patiently at Daisy's side. "We were just passing through, traveling to Alder Castle."

Holt and Connor exchange a nod in greeting.

"Did something happen at the palace?" Holt asks.

I nod. "We found traitors among members of the guard. It was too dangerous for me to stay."

"What about Beth?" he asks, a hint of concern in his voice.

Guilt gnaws at me. "I will send for her as soon as I can," I assure him.

"Good," he says, flashing a relieved smile. "Well, would you like to come in? James isn't home, but his mother is. She's cooking some—"

I put a hand on his arm. "I'm sorry, but time is short, we really must be going." Holt's face crumples, and I can't help but feel terrible.

"I wish I could stay, I really do, but there's an urgent matter we must bring up to the king," I explain, hoping he will understand. He is quiet for a moment, brow furrowed as he entertains a thought.

"I could come with you?" he asks abruptly, sounding eager. I blink at him, stunned.

"To Alder Castle?" I stammer.

He nods excitedly, biting his lip. "Yes. I could find work there."

"Are you not happy here?" I shoot a quick glance at the cottage.

"You know me, princess." He shrugs. "Country life just isn't for me."

My eyes dart to the dirt-smeared gloves and the tattered, peasant garments he wears, a drastic change from a wine bearer's uniform. "Besides," he adds with a smile, "You and Beth will be there. It will be just like old times."

"I..." I start, looking over my shoulder at Connor, who is watching intently, but makes no sign to his thoughts. "I would be happy to have you."

He claps his hands, beaming mischievously. "Great."

"Wait," Connor pipes in. "Before you decide, know that it might be dangerous; there are men searching for us." I had forgotten about Elijah, I realize. After spending all those days at Jessamine's farm, I felt as though that threat was no longer an issue, especially now that we have crossed the Alderian border, where the cities are under constant watch. But Elijah is a madman.

"All the more reason to tag along," Holt answers, eager and

confident. I, on the other hand, am no longer certain that I want him to come.

"Are you sure? I could send for you, along with Beth," I offer.

"Listen, I might not look the part, but I can hold my own. And if there is a chance you two might get into trouble, I want to be there to help."

I sigh. "All right, fine. You may accompany us, but with one condition: I get my horse back."

"Done!" he says immediately.

Smiling, I shake my head at Holt. "Well then, are you ready to go?"

Holt opens his mouth as if to speak but pauses. "I don't suppose you could wait for me to pack a few things?"

Chapter Twenty-one

James' mother is not pleased. Her wrathful voice bellows through the cottage.

"You bawdy troll!"

Holt comes bolting out the front door, a bulging satchel slung across his torso. James' mother storms after him, waving a pitchfork in the air. She is a stout, brawny woman, and looks rather odd under the simple red dress she wears over a white shirt of rolled sleeves and a ruffled neck. The angry color on her face matches the crimson dress. She is distracted for a moment, noticing Connor and me, but she quickly resumes her ranting.

"I gave you food, a place to stay, and this is how you repay me?" she growls.

"But what of the garden, madam? I—"

"You think that's payment? You ruined my vegetables, you whelp!" She charges at Holt like an angry bull, pitchfork raised, but he whirls out of the way before she can strike at him.

"Uh, Meredith? A little help here?" Holt asks.

I grimace, not exactly sure that I can be of help. "Madam," I call out gingerly. I fall on deaf ears. The woman is unrelenting in her chase, determined to get at Holt, who is now running around in circles.

Beside me, Connor gives an aggravated sigh. "We don't have time for this," he mutters. He steps in, swift and blunt, coming up behind the woman to pluck the pitchfork out of her thrashing arm. She stumbles back, but as her gaze falls on Connor, her confusion knits into a scowl.

"You give that back this instant or I swear—" she doesn't get to finish. Connor bends backward, his arm coiling and uncoiling as he hurls it across the field. The pitchfork becomes a faint shadow, its descent barely visible in the distance.

The woman's eyes protrude from their sockets. She curls her lips at Connor, and for a moment, I think she is about to pounce on him. But she seems to reconsider, her stance softening slightly. "You better be gone when I return with that pitchfork, lest you fancy I stab you with it." Then she whirls on Holt. "The same goes for you, scoundrel. I never want to see your face again."

"That went well," Holt quips when she is out of earshot.

I chuckle, watching James' mother chase after the pitchfork. "I don't think she likes you, Holt."

"Old Agnes adores me; she's just having a bad day." Holt winks.

We leave without looking back. The clear, open road soon becomes an enclosed path that cuts into the trees, scattering sunlight in patches of light throughout the canopy. Shrouded in woodland, the crisp air smells of bark and damp clay. Hidden birds coo and flap their wings through the trees, rustling the leaves as we canter by. Holt does his best to keep up, but Daisy is a smaller horse, nowhere near as strong as Diago, and she tires more easily. Every once in a while we have to slow down a bit so that he can catch up. Part of me feels guilty for bringing him along, but another part of me is glad that he is here. Beth and I had dolefully given him up for good, thinking we would never meet again; she will be in for a quite a pleasant surprise when she arrives with Anabella, which I am hoping will be soon.

As the day dwindles by and the light begins to fade, we set up camp in the forest where the undergrowth is sparse and manageable. Connor decides against hunting for dinner and uses our rations instead. Surrounded by brambles and ferns, we hunker down on a fallen, moss-covered log to share sundried meat and pecans, eating in fatigued silence. I chew quickly though, not liking the way the overly salted meat dries my tongue. It's not until we pull out the wine that Holt springs back to life with renewed vigor.

"I'm sorry to say, the wine at the palace pales in comparison to Far Water wine," he brags, holding up the leather canteen to his appraising eyes.

"Not that it matters; we don't live there anymore," I point out somberly, surprised at the nostalgia that catches in my throat.

He takes a mouthful from the canteen. "Good point." He cranes his neck at Connor. "What's the wine like at Alder castle?"

"They carriage the wine from Far Water," Connor says, his voice distant. He sits next to me. Our shoulders and hands softly brush against each other, and yet he feels so far away. He stares into the encroaching dusk, his eyebrows knitted with distress. I wish I could give him some reassurance. If only we were alone, I would reach out to him. But I don't feel comfortable exposing my feelings to Holt, or anyone else, for that matter. My knees quiver at the thought of having to speak to King Perceval about it. But that is something I will worry about later. I discreetly lift a finger and caress the back of Connor's hand. He looks down at the gesture, his fingers responding in kind.

Holt peels himself from the log, groaning his way back to his feet. "Did you two hear that?"

I feel Connor go still under my touch. I, too, sit suddenly tense, my ears perking up to the sounds of the forest. I hone in on the chirring of insects and the rustle of animals in the under-brush.

"Hear what?" I whisper.

He lifts his arms over his head into a stretch. "The sound of nature calling. I will be right back." Smirking, Holt hands me the canteen.

I let out a drawn out breath, glaring at Holt's back as he drifts away into the wilderness and disappears from view.

Connor removes the strapped bow and quiver and slips out of his jerkin. "Here," he says, bunching it up into ball. I slowly reach for it, confused.

"What is this for?" I ask.

"Pillow."

"What about you?"

He stands and draws out a sword. "I will keep watch; there might be boars out there."

"Want some company?" I offer.

"You need to rest."

I place the balled-up jerkin on the log and pull up beside him, crossing my arms at my chest. "As do you."

"I'll be fine."

I frown at the iciness of his tone. "I worry about them too, you know," I say, holding back the frustration from my voice. "But we have to hope for the best, it's the only way to keep going."

He gives a slight shake of his head. "You should also prepare for the worst.

"I don't see how that helps. Just because you expect pain does not mean it will hurt any less."

He looks at me, his eyes searching and probing for something. "It makes it easier to live with the pain." He speaks with certainty, as though from experience, but every part of me refuses to agree, feeling as though it would be no different than giving up.

"No. As long as there is a chance, I will believe in it, and I hold on to it."

He sighs. "And what will you do if the king denies our requests?" he asks softly, his voice almost a whisper.

"I…" Somehow the words get lodged in my throat.

"I have faith in my king; he will help my aunt. But you and I, that's a different matter. His blessing will mean nothing unless he is willing to uphold the alliance. As much as I would like to, I can't promise he will consent. You have to be prepared for that," he says, his voice solemn with a steely resolve.

I swallow the hurt that swells within me.

"I understand," I say, fighting back the sting of tears.

At this, his face softens a little. "Meredith..." He finds my hand and draws me to him. He leans in, touching his temple to mine, and whispers, "It doesn't mean I'm giving up. I will fight for you."

"Then I will hold on to hope," I whisper back.

My lips are reaching for his when we hear Holt's steady approach through the snapping of branches and crunching of leaves. I grudgingly pull away, ready to glare at Holt once more, but I am stopped short by a sudden coldness that numbs me to the core.

Even in the inky blackness of shadows, I still make out the wickedly satisfied smile on Elijah's face.

"Well, isn't this touching?"

Chapter Twenty-two

Elijah's men filter in through the moon-speckled darkness, the silver light glinting off the blades of their swords. Connor pushes me back, unsheathing his other sword from the scabbard, now wielding a weapon in each hand. Part of me wants to tell him to lower his defenses, to give myself over and ask them to let him go. It's me they are after. Connor is only an obstacle. If only I believed Elijah would allow Connor to leave unharmed, I would do it.

"I like your spirit, soldier," Elijah says to Connor. "I was very impressed with your skills the night of the ball. You successfully took on five of my men. That was quite a feat. You wouldn't be interested in switching employers, would you?"

He takes Connor's silence with a disappointed shrug. "Well then, boys, get on with it," he says.

The lot of his men, eight in total, step forward in a cluster. Connor won't stand a chance. I have to help him. Pulse rising, I snatch Connor's bow away from the bed of leaves, slinging the quiver across my back as I've seen him do so many times. I struggle with my shaking hands to rest the arrow on the bow, trying to remember what Connor taught me. Somehow, I manage to do it. I pull the string back as far as it allows, feeling the tips of my fingers go white with effort.

Connor stands ready, his arms taut, waiting for the first move. I glance over at Elijah, sickened by the notion that he really seems to be enjoying himself, nonchalantly perched up against the trunk of a tree with his feet crossed, as though expecting a grand performance.

In the end, only two of the men charge. They come at us, swords swinging, and I'm strangled with fear for Connor. But where these men show aggression and ruthlessness, Connor responds with cool-headed precision. He moves, nimble and deadly, parrying blows with his swords. He kicks the feet from under one soldier and disarms the other with a swift thrust of his sword. His arm slashes sideways, and blood seeps from the unarmed soldier's neck. The one on the ground is getting back up, as two others pounce forward.

Shoulders tight, I aim at one of the charging men. My breath bursts in and out of me as my fingers release the arrow. The blur of speed pierces the soldier's thigh. If I weren't gripped with fear, I would probably flash a victorious smile. The man growls in agony, his hands clutching at the lodged arrow. Then he breaks it in two, leaving the one half protruding from his leg. He bellows a deafening battle cry and forges on, limping, his furious stare pinned on me just as two more soldiers charge at us.

I fumble for another arrow, ignoring the panic that tightens my muscles. Out of the corner of my eye, I see the injured soldier pick up speed. I tell myself to hurry, but my hands are too jerky. Gritting my teeth, I manage to place the arrow on the rest, but as I try to position my fingers around the shaft, my grip loosens and the arrow falls to my feet. I hear his rushing stomps, growling his way toward me. *No time*, I think, grasping behind me for another arrow as he swings his sword. I hold back a scream. But as the blade comes slicing down, Connor swoops in, deflecting it's descent with a metallic clang. In tandem, his other arm comes up, plunging a sword into the soldier's chest.

The other soldiers come together behind Connor, their attacks unrelenting. Connor swivels back to block one sword, and a second, the clashing of metal blending with a cacophony of heavy breaths. Then, there is a third strike, one that Connor fails to intercept. It slices across his abdomen, leaving a dark, wet trail across his shirt.

I scream, my heart leaping out of my chest. I hear Connor strain against the next attacks, thwarting them, but just barely, as he struggles to get his bearings. Fear and anger course through me. Then a single-minded focus takes over: save Connor. I take yet another arrow, but this time I lunge with it. I stab the closest soldier in the neck, and try not to flinch when I feel the sharp point of the arrow digging deep.

The soldier takes a haggard step back, clamping a hand around the wound. Dark blood trickles through his fingers. My stomach heaves at the raw iron smell of it. He stares at me, wide-eyed, as though he can't believe he has just been defeated by a girl. With a final wheeze, he collapses onto the leaves and broken branches.

A new wave of soldiers is now rushing at Connor, leaving Elijah to watch in solitude. I don't know why he doesn't join his men, but I am grateful for it; Connor has his hands full with the four that remain, flanked on all sides. None of them come at me however, focusing their group effort to take Connor down. They are mistaken if they think I'm just going to stand by and watch. I take aim, but it's hard to set a target from the clustered lot of shifting shadows. My resolve falters, afraid that I might hit Connor by accident. I groan inwardly, desperation seeping through my brow in beads of sweat. I am wasting precious time.

And then my fear surges once again when I hear Connor gasp in pain.

Before I can do anything though, I feel a sharp pain at my side. I reel back, and Elijah's face looms before me.

He smiles. "What's the matter, princess? Sore spot?"

I feel the hair at the nape of my neck prickle. I press a hand down at the wound right above my hip, wincing at the spiking pain.

"Let us finish what we started, shall we?" Elijah croons, stepping closer.

I recoil from his nearness, hobbling away as my gaze lingers on the blood-stained dagger in his hand. My heart thrashes in my ears, and I start to feel as though the forest is closing in, ensnaring me to Elijah's morbid design. But despite my fear, my lips pull back, baring teeth.

"You're a monster."

Elijah chuckles, eyes glowing in the moonlight. "Monster, huh? I like it."

Without warning, he charges. I am about to break into a run when a shadow smashes into him from the side. They careen through the underbrush, grunting over the snaps of twigs and the crackle of disturbed leaves.

"Run," comes Holt's strangled voice.

My legs twitch, ready to oblige, a pure survival instinct. But

I can't leave Holt to deal with Elijah by himself. He is no match for him. I drop the bow, fearful of wasting more time with my aim. In the end I do run, just not in the direction Holt was hoping I would. I race toward them, ignoring the pain on my side, and the wet, oozing blood that crawls down my leg. I scramble for an arrow, readying the tip between my clammy fingers. As I near them, I catch the glint of Elijah's dagger, hovering just above Holt's chest. Holt is fighting him, straining to push him off. A trickle of icy fear congeals my blood.

"Get away from him!" I bellow.

I clutch the arrowhead so tight I feel the sting from its sharp edges. My hands ache to use it, to pierce through Elijah's ruthless, manic heart and send him to the pits of hell. But I don't make it. Lurching to a stop, I watch in horror as Elijah wins the struggle, driving his dagger into Holt's chest.

Chapter Twenty-three

"No!" I cry out, my hands clapping over my ears in sheer disbelief.

I am paralyzed, frozen, my legs rooted to forest floor. Holt's eyes stare blankly at the patches of night sky that filter through the trees, his lips slightly parted.

Elijah lunges. I choke on a sob as he crashes into me. His body nails me to the ground with utter violence, knocking the wind out of my lungs. Before I can catch a breath, his fingers dig into my side. Hot, searing pain cripples me, and I let out an earsplitting howl. But he doesn't relent, and the agonizing pain begins to cloud my vision. Then, abruptly, he stops. I gasp with relief.

Elijah laughs, casual and apathetic. "Oh, it's not over, princess, not yet. By the time I am done with you, you'll be begging for—"

Heavy, fast-approaching steps distract him. He jerks his head at the sound and darts to his feet. Connor pummels into Elijah with bare hands, smashing him against the nearest tree. Connor's hands lock around Elijah's neck, growling with a rage that gives me pause. I watch him strangle Elijah, feeling both glad and unsettled, waiting with bated breath for it all to end.

Then Elijah thrusts his dagger into the back of Connor's hand. Connor snarls, and his grip loosens enough for Elijah to take the offensive, swinging the blade at him.

Connor blocks it, taking the cut of the dagger in his forearm. Then Connor slams his elbow to the side of Elijah's face. He recovers quickly though, returning with a fist in Connor's jaw. In the split second that it takes Connor to regain his balance, Elijah tackles him to the ground.

A dark hunger for Elijah's death overwhelms my senses. I feel blood pounding in my head, my vision turning red, and my fear all but gone. With the arrow still in my grasp, I move to finish what I had started. In an instant, I am at the foot of their scuffle. Elijah has Connor pinned to the ground, and just as with Holt, he presses his dagger against him, visibly shaking with the effort to lower the blade. But unlike Holt, Connor is able to hold him off, their arms and hands locked in a standstill.

This is my chance. I swing my arm down, the arrow hissing through the air, closing the distance to the back of Elijah's neck.

He dodges the blow with uncanny precision, snatching my wrist in a crushing hold. I watch, helpless, as his other arm swoops up with the dagger. The pointed blade angles for my throat, toting death like a signature. I can't think nor flinch. In that split second, all I can do is stare at it, breathless. But the course of the dagger errs, burying deep into the inside of my shoulder instead. I am so overwrought with tension, however, that I can't even feel the lodged blade. Elijah doesn't get the chance to pull it out. Connor has already wrenched him away, dragging him back in a chokehold.

Bile rises in my throat. I feel weak, but I force myself to remain upright, worried that I might blackout. With nervous fingers, I clasp onto the dagger's handle. I lock my jaw, preparing for the pain that will follow. But Connor's strained voice stops me.

"Don't. You'll bleed more."

He looks as exhausted as he sounds. My heart shrinks to see him so drained and weak. His body has taken a severe beating, but how grave are his wounds? I privately curse the shade of the night for its concealing veil. Still, Connor does not give up. Elijah fights against his hold, legs thrashing to regain the advantage, his eyes wild and menacing. I have no intention of waiting around for him to do so.

"I will kill him with it," I hiss, unwilling, my fingers still fastened to the dagger.

I am certain Connor would have denied me once more, if he could, and perhaps I would have listened. But the decision is made for me when Elijah twists under Connor's strangling arms, rolling out of his hold. I pull the dagger out with a yelp, and the blood comes gushing out. I ignore it.

I take a step forward, blinking rapidly, trying to clear my fuzzy sight, when a whistle cuts through the air. Diago comes into view. The horse trots up and stops just a few paces away. He snorts as though uncomfortable with the commotion. Defiance bursts out of me in droves.

"No," I blurt out, though the protest comes weak and sluggish.

The scuffle, too, sounds strange. Their grunting and panting has slowed to a crawl, the voices blended into one. I recognize the signs, and I realize my consciousness is slipping. I grip on to it like a vise, refusing to give in. But with each breath I take, I feel less and less in control.

Suddenly, the ground shifts from under me. It feels as though I am floating. And I smell blood. Not mine. Someone else's, mixed with a familiar scent. I think I hear myself say his name. I open my eyes, searching, but I can't see anything, save for a distant blur of forest. I feel something squeeze around my waist, securing me in place, and a touch of warmth at my cheek. A soft, fleeting brush that speaks words I cannot hear. But the warmth leaves me, replaced by a cool breeze. I find it refreshing against the layer of moisture that covers my skin, enlivening almost, even as I give myself over to the comfort of the dark.

Chapter Twenty-four

My sluggish lids flutter to a slanted ceiling. Dusty wood panels recede toward me, held together by four carved logs. Blackened walls of stone line the room, lit by the dancing glow of candles and a small fireplace. To my right is a tub. A folded towel lies limp over its edge. I wait for a recollection to materialize, to remember where I am, but in my half-lidded stupor, all I sense are the dull aches in my body.

I fall in and out of sleep. The memories meld together without order. I am vaguely aware that I am sleeping, though I am never fully awake. Once, I see a woman wiping at my arms with a wet cloth. There is also a man in a guard's attire. He paces around my bed with a sword at his belt. But for the most part, I see flashes of an empty room that keeps me warm and isolated.

Eventually, I wake up.

I sit up with a gasp, feeling as though I have slumbered for years. A stinging pain sears my shoulder and below my waist.

"Connor?" I croak, though there is no one there to hear.

What happened?

I pick at my brain for answers, but what I find is the last thing I want to remember.

Holt.

The back of my throat contracts with pain as grief threatens to burst out of me. I hold it back with a deep breath, pressing my palms at the pool of unshed tears that well up in my eyes. I shut out the horrid memory of Holt's last moments and center my thoughts on the present. Glancing down at my bandaged shoulder, my eyes trail down to the clean chemise I wear. I raise my arm, tuck my nose against it and take a deep breath. A floral, minty ointment scent saturates my skin. Someone has been taking great care to nurse me back to health. But who?

There is only one way to find out.

I push my legs to stand. At once, I feel the effects of being bedridden for too long. My vision goes white for a moment, knees wobbling as I try to balance on feeble feet. I lay a hand on the plush bedding to steady myself. Taking small steps, I make my way across the room to find a short set of stairs that lead to a door.

I lumber up the steps and try the knob. It turns in my hand without restraint. I nudge the door open, casting a furtive glance at the abrupt corridor that turns a sharp corner. A golden light coming from another room paints the walls with warmth. I hear voices, low and indistinct, engaged in relaxed conversation.

When I step in, however, the room quiets to abrupt silence. A group of guards congregates on an L-shaped table. A fireplace recedes into the length of the wall behind them. Men both young and old peer at me. Some have full-grown beards, others are clean shaven, while a few sport short-trimmed stubbles. They wear the familiar Alder uniform with the lion crest over their chainmail shirts.

Understanding begins to dawn on me. This must be a military outpost.

"Where is Connor?" I ask the lot of stunned faces.

Several brows shoot up and looks of concern stir within the room. But before any of them answer, the woman I'd seen tending to me walks in. She almost drops the bread-filled tray in her hands.

"Goodness, child," she chides, setting the tray on the table. She crosses the room in haste, using her body like a wall, blocking me to the rest of the room. "Let's get you dressed first," she says in a hushed voice.

I know I should oblige her. It's the least I can do. But there is a crevice within my chest that fills with dread, and I can't shake the feeling away.

"Where is Connor?" I demand, refusing to move.

The woman gives me a sympathetic look. "You were alone when we found you," she whispers. "It was just you and your horse."

"Horse?" I murmur, questioning my memories. Did I leave Connor behind? No, I couldn't have.

"A black horse," the woman adds, noticing my confusion.

Her words turn my stomach to ice. Connor is out there, wounded. Maker knows how badly.

I grasp her arms. "Please, we have to find him. He's hurt."

"Madam," says the dark-haired, mustached guard who approaches. "Was it Connor Westwend who was with you?"

My eyes widen at the mention of his name. "Yes! How did you know? Have you found him?"

A dark shadow settles in his expression. "We found a pile of burned bodies out in the woods. We searched for survivors but there were only some weapons left behind, and a few horses roaming around."

Burned? I wonder with disgust. Who could have...?

I shake my head. No. Elijah has to be dead. For him to have survived would mean that Connor...I swallow the rest of that thought, unwilling to form the words. I cannot afford to think like that. Connor is a survivor, I remind myself. Jessamine said so herself.

"Here." The guard motions to someone at the table. "The swords were either bent or broken, but it looks like this made it out unscathed." He gestures at the hands of the guard who inches up to us.

The sight cuts to my very soul.

I reach for the bow, my mind racing for an explanation. *He left it behind*, urges the tiny voice in my head. But as much as I want to believe that, I know I am just lying to myself. My feet disappear, and I plunge to my knees like dead weight. Unconsciously, my fingers curve around the bow. I want to throw up. My chest shakes and heaves, choking me with an endless wave of sobs. Connor is dead. Thrown into a pile and burned. I want to scream until the pain stops. But each moment is worse than the one before it. I drift farther and farther into a yawning black hole. It swallows me whole, drowning me in it, until I am no longer.

Chapter Twenty-five

I am a cold, withering shadow. My heart, a heavy lump in my chest, is wilted and decayed. Numb, soaked in disbelief, I build up a wall, a calloused barricade.

Four of the guards from the outpost lead the way to Alder Castle. After managing to extract information from me, they promptly decided to take me to King Perceval. There was a change in their manner upon learning my identity, seeming nervous to be in charge of a princess' safety, or as I heard one of them whisper, their future queen.

I keep close all the things I have left to hold dear. I ride on Diago, with Connor's bow snug at my back. And Daisy, one of the horses found in the woods, follows in step without a rider.

Seeing her at the outpost's stable had brought a bit of solace to my grief. Sharing a roof with a group of strangers, she had been a welcome shoulder to cry on. I grip on to her reins, even though I know it's unnecessary; wherever I go, she will follow. Regardless, I feel better with the reins under my clutch. We push through dreary skies that hint of storms, but rain never comes. In spite of setting up camp every evening, nights and days blur together and I scarcely notice the passage of time. At some point, I notice the terrain has drastically changed. Somewhere along the way, the longleaf pines were replaced with thick spruce trees; the flat landscape now a mesh of mountains.

"Your highness," I hear a guard say. I don't have to look up. I can smell the food he offers. Silently groaning, I ignore him. Eating has become a chore. An unpleasant necessity.

"Please, you must eat," he says quietly after a moment. I keep silent, but apparently he is the stubborn kind. "I'm Lief, by the way."

Go away.

He doesn't. My eyes flick to the young guard. His face, capped by short, blonde curls, is tender, and too young for a guard, I think. He holds two bowls of cooked vegetables, one in each hand. The thought of chewing makes me sick, but I reach for a bowl. The steam hits my nose. It smells of bland carrots and potatoes, boiled and unseasoned. I mindlessly mash them together into a mushy blend of orange and yellow.

Now that I've had time to sort out my thoughts, I remember a question that remained unanswered by the mustached guard, whom everyone referred to as Captain.

"How did the captain know about Connor?" I ask Lief, speaking for the first time since we left.

Lief's face perks up at my voice, surprise etched on his youthful features. *Just how old is he, fifteen?*

"The horse," he says, gulping down food. "We mark the shoes with an insignia. We knew it belonged to one of our men, but we didn't know who until you came out asking about him."

I feel a frown creep into my brow. I distinctly remember mentioning only his given name. "Is Connor a rare name in Alder?"

Lief gives me a curious look. "No. But Sir Westwend was a widely recognized soldier." Then his eyes fall in a forlorn gesture. "I always hoped I would make his acquaintance. Was he as great as everyone painted him to be?"

Was. The word cuts like a jagged knife. I still cannot fathom that he and Holt are gone. It's like an impossible truth; you know it's real and yet your mind refuses to believe it.

"I don't know how everyone else painted him," I say, doing my best to keep my voice from breaking. "But he was unlike anyone else I have ever met."

Lief observes me, a hesitant look crossing his face. "I found something back there. I believe it's his."

My attention stirs and I stare at him, expectant and anxious.

He removes his satchel, producing a dark, rolled up fabric from it. He hands it to me. "I thought you might like to have it. If it is his, I mean."

His jerkin. I hold back a sob and lick my dry, trembling lips.

"Thank you," I whisper, tucking the jerking underneath my arm. I return my attention to the bowl of food, desperately needing a distraction to keep the tears from coming.

Lief doesn't say anything else, content to see me eating too. There was no need for him to insist though, we both knew I would eventually have a few spoonfuls. Albeit, the food would surely be cold by then, but that doesn't make much difference to me now. Nothing does. Except for revenge. For Connor and for Holt. It's the only thing that holds me now. I will kill Elijah, if it's the last thing I do. No matter the cost. Though I have not forgotten about the Borderlands, but it has become just an afterthought now, a task I must ensure is taken care of.

Back at the outpost, I had insisted on accompanying the guards in their search parties. I wanted to be present when they found Elijah. But there was no trace of him anywhere, and that only served to fuel my hatred. It's easier this way. I prefer to revel in bitterness than to drown in sorrow.

And that is how I spend my traveling days. I keep to myself, and the guards have enough sense to leave me be, save for Lief, who is far too kind for his own good.

But it's not until I lay eyes on the walls of Alder Castle that I realize just how much time has passed. The structure emerges like a mountain, colossal and domineering. It towers over Alder City with an imperial air. The day is cold and damp here, a clear indication of harsh winters. My haggard dress clings to my skin. I mindlessly stroke Diago while I watch the guards exchange words with the men stationed at the city gates. Their curious attention flicks to me as they speak. Even after we are allowed in, I feel their eyes follow me. The city is majestic. Uniform buildings of white walls and blue-gray slate roofs populate the cobblestone streets. Together they form a perfectly structured maze that stirs with life. In similar fashion to Far Water, and all those other towns and villages we passed through these last two weeks, guards patrol the area.

An ample river that feeds into a lake separates the castle from the rest of the city, creating a natural moat. A bridge stretches across it, gates on each end. The first gate opens the path across the bridge. The other leads through the outer wall of the castle. Again, we must seek permission to proceed. But the guards at this gate are more cautious.

"Step forward," calls one of them, motioning for me after

speaking with the guard that leads our party.

I gently tug at the reins and saunter up to the gate. The guard, clad in breastplate and chain mail, gives me a suspicious once-over. But then a sharpness comes to his expression as he inspects Diago. "Is that Sir Westwend's horse?"

The sound of his name is like whiplash.

"Yes," I say through the lump in my throat.

Concern creases his brow, but he says nothing else. He walks away and out of view. Shortly after, the heavy scraping of metal announces our admittance.

A whole town could fit inside the castle walls. Expansive fields of trimmed grass and bushes surround the mighty structure. The castle is a monument, easily three times the size of Stonefall Palace. And their facades could not be any more different. Where Stonefall Palace is snowy white and polished, Alder Castle is stone gray and rustic, with green layers of moss hugging its walls. The tall double doors at the entrance stand wide open, spewing a path of loose gravel that cuts through the grass in sharp angles, creating three separate sections at its threshold. A fountain of enormous diameter is planted inside one of them. People walk to and from the castle doors, mingling among merchants and traders with carts of rich-colored textiles, jewelry, and other items of luxury. The buzz of conversation is wide reaching.

It's a much larger court than what I am accustomed to. Then again, everything here is larger.

We trot over to the stables, where I find myself struggling to part from Diago. I know my fear is nonsensical. I would see the horse again. But nevertheless, it proves rather difficult to dismount, as though I'm separating from the only thing I have left of Connor. *You still have his bow*, I remind myself. And I hold onto it, squeezing it tight, making my hands ache.

"Daisy will keep you company," I murmur to the horse, petting him briefly before walking away.

Inside the castle, we are escorted through a dark hallway of barrel-vaulted ceilings. Standing candelabras light the way. The echo of voices grows louder and louder until we reach their source. We enter a large chamber with a row of arched, stained windows and a coffered ceiling. An assembly of people blocks our view of someone speaking.

"...it's been our family home for generations. We humbly plead that you may spare it."

A petitions chamber.

The four guards urge me to follow as they break through the awaiting crowd. Lief looks back a few times to send reassuring smiles my way.

"Baron, you have been rewarded generously for your troubles. I suggest you—" The king, a well-aged man with shoulder-length gray hair and a matching beard, stops mid-sentence.

"What is the meaning of this?" he demands, clearly displeased. Up a couple of stone steps is the throne, where the king sits next to a gracefully poised woman with a crown atop her combed golden-brown hair. The queen. At his other side, a few steps back, stands a handsome young man with fair features. That must be the prince. Ethan. It feels strange to finally put a face to the name I have known my entire life. My eyes stay on him as the captain explains.

"Your majesty, we've journeyed from the Ironforge Outpost, just outside of Far Water, to deliver Princess Meredith of Stonefall." At the mention of my name, the captain suddenly garners Ethan's undivided attention. He takes two steps forward, bringing his hand to rest at the back of the king's throne. In an instant, his searching gaze settles on me, and our eyes meet. Neither of us looks away.

"Who gave the order to bring the princess here?" the king asks.

"We found her, sire; she was wounded. Connor Westwend was escorting her here, but they were attacked by soldiers of Talos."

After a moment of confused pause, the king asks, "And where is Connor?"

I shut my eyes, forcing back the tears that prickle my eyes.

"Dead...your majesty," the guard says with solemn hesitation.

A wave of stunned silence crashes through the room. The queen's hands fly up to her mouth in horror.

"Lies!" Ethan protests.

The king's mouth moves as he whispers something to his son. But whatever cautionary words he speaks are not enough to dissuade the prince. Seeming determined, Ethan descends the steps and crosses the room to stand face to face with the captain.

"What proof do you have?" he asks through gritted teeth.

While the captain stumbles for a reply, I seize the moment and step forth. There are many things I could say. Where he died, or by whose hand. But the ghastly words remain locked inside me. Instead, I produce Connor's bow. I present it to Ethan with open palms, praying he won't snatch it away. If he does, I fear I will come undone and crumble to pieces.

He doesn't take it. He swallows and stares at it in silence. Surprised, I watch as his eyes turn to glass. Palpable pain inscribes the lines of his face, his mouth pressed into a taut line. There is a subtle trembling in his chin.

Then suddenly, he wheels back to face the throne, his hands clenched tightly at his sides. "Father, we must avenge him."

"That would be considered an act of war," the king gently explains.

"War has already been declared by their own actions," Ethan says bitterly.

King Perceval shakes his head. "They have done no such thing."

I flinch at Ethan's scream. "He was family!"

I can't even grasp the impact of his words before the king responds. "Not by blood."

Standing right behind Ethan, I can see the shaking rage that ripples through him. "You will deny me this?" he asks slowly, in a seething, low voice.

The king's response rings like a warning. "Son, we will continue this in private."

Ethan is silent in his rage, locked in a challenging stare with his father.

"Ethan, please," says the queen, coming out of her stricken silence. The relationship between the two shines in that moment. Ethan's shoulders soften. And without a word, he turns, brushing past me, disappearing through the parting crowd of wide-eyed faces.

Chapter Twenty-six

The water of the lake chills the gentle breeze. Below me, a group of ducks swim and quack loudly to each other by the bank. Occasionally, a bird flies by, gliding with open wings. It's soothingly peaceful. But its tranquility does not settle me. Turmoil lives inside me. And at present, my thoughts stagger to grasp what they have just learned. Connor was loved by the royal family. He was important to them. Just how important, I do not know, though it seems he was closest to the prince. The question I asked Connor at the ball comes back to me.

Will I like him?

Yes.

Connor had not just been a faithful soldier to his prince.

He'd been his friend. Why did he not tell me? Did he not trust me? A doleful pang digs deep into my chest. But now I understand why he believed he could speak to the king about us, why he thought he might consent. And by the looks of it, he may have.

I'd only just found him, and now he is gone, taken from me in the cruelest of ways. I will never again see those eyes. Never again will I feel his arms around me. The hardest part is knowing that I will never get the chance to tell him that I love him. A truth I'd known all along. An instinct that took hold of my thoughts; my body; my heart.

I don't turn at the sound of footsteps. Ethan walks up beside me. "Madam," he says, taking my hand to kiss it. "I wish we could have met under different circumstances." He is a completely composed version of the man I saw at the petitions chamber only hours ago. He smiles softly at me, but the gesture does not reach his dulled chestnut eyes.

I nod. "I've called you here because I have a favor to ask...on Connor's behalf. My intentions were to bring the matter to the king, but in light of what transpired at the petitions chamber, I believe it is you I should I speak with."

His eyes sharpen. "I'm listening."

I begin by recounting the events at the palace, from the poisoned wine to the night of the ball, and our findings of the royal guard being compromised. Then I tell him about Jessamine and her farm, the dire situation of the Borderlands, and Connor's plan to help them. Ethan listens quietly, his eyes never wandering.

"I will speak to my father," he says, pausing. Then he adds, "Thank you."

"It's the least I can do for him," I say with a hard swallow.

"And it will be done," he reassures me.

I cock my head to the side, glancing up at him from under my lashes. "I gather you two were close friends?" I probe.

"Connor was a brother to me."

I feel my throat squeeze. I swallow but it doesn't go away. "He never told me any of this," I blurt out with unintentional resentment. And I wince. Did he notice?

A rueful smile tugs at the corner of his mouth. "He was under oath."

My eyes narrow. "Under oath?"

Ethan sighs. He looks at me then. "I was hoping to tell you this when I got to know you a little better. As you are aware, our fathers have not seen eye to eye for the past ten years, and we—"

"I wasn't aware," I correct him.

He blinks, clearly surprised.

"I know the alliance is falling apart, but I was never told any of the particulars," I clarify.

"I see," he says, seeming to draw his own conclusions. Connor had said King Perceval was different, that he wasn't like my father, and perhaps that's why I sense surprise in Ethan. Perhaps here I won't be kept in the dark.

"Well, you and I must have a talk soon, but for now let's just say our fathers have different...ideals, when it comes to matters of state," he says.

My father's ideals leave much to be desired, I gather.

"The continued prosperity of my kingdom is dependent on its rulers. For generations, my family has ensured that those destined for the throne were fit to rule. Given the bad blood between our fathers, we weren't convinced that you would be up to the task. To tell you the truth, my father was ready to break off the alliance and annul the marriage contract, but my mother thought we should give you a chance.

"And so we did. When my father learned your life was in danger, he offered to postpone breaking the alliance with the condition that Connor was hired as your personal escort."

"I'm assuming you are about to tell me how keeping me safe has anything to do with me being fit to rule?" I ask.

"Connor was there to protect you, yes, but he was also there to make out your character," he says carefully.

With a will of its own, my mouth falls open. I remember Connor studying me. How much he kept from me. He'd been judging me, all that time, testing my integrity.

But if that's what he was doing, why would he...?

A slither of doubt uncoils within me. Was it even real? Or was it just a set up? A cruel trap to prove me unfit to rule? For the very first time, I feel that solid foundation of trust waver. But my bruised, wilted heart beats with denial, incapable of believing such a vile truth. And yet, the question lingers, clasping on to my chest, refusing to be buried.

"Is something the matter?" Ethan asks, reading my expression.

I ignore the question. "So what happens now?" I manage to ask with a steady voice. "What will become of the alliance?"

Ethan's expression softens. "He sacrificed his life to save yours; that tells me all I need to know."

I fight the confused tears that demand to well up in my eyes. I repress the urge to give in to the pain that threatens to wreck me. I can't let him see. I can't let anyone see.

"It was his job," I say.

"No. He is—was protective by nature, but not altruistic; Connor would not have risked his life for you if he didn't deem you worthy of it," he says, his voice vehement.

"I...gather the king had a high regard for his opinion," I say, surprised that my voice doesn't crack.

He lowers his gaze. When he speaks, his voice is somber.

"We all did."

"I'm sorry," I whisper, though I'm not sure which of us I say it to.

When Ethan looks up at me, I see violence in his eyes. "I will find the ones responsible. One way or another, I will make them pay."

Yes, Elijah will pay for all that he has taken from me. It won't bring them back. And it won't ease my suffering. But we will have justice.

"I know just who you're looking for."

He nods, seeming grateful.

"On one condition," I add.

He arches an eyebrow but waits for my response.

I straighten, feeling my chest rise with conviction.

"Teach me how to fight."

Epilogue

Pain. It throbs like the toll of a bell against my skull. The more aware I am of it, the more I feel it.

"Did you see that, Father? I think he's coming to," says a gentle voice.

I open my eyes to walls. A room. The light of a window. Two people seated before me.

"How are you feeling?" asks the gentle voice. A young woman. Her features sharpen into view. I can see her now. Black hair. Bright green eyes. Unfamiliar. I try to gauge my situation. Bandages are wrapped around my exposed torso. My ribs ache.

"He's still dazed from the medicine," says another voice. An elderly man.

Medicine? "What did you give me?" I croak.

"For the pain," the girl explains.

"What happened to me?" I ask, unable to recall how I managed to get here.

They exchange a look. "You don't remember?" the girl asks.

I shake my head, which shoots a stab of pain at the back of my head.

"What do you remember?" the old man asks.

I scour my thoughts for memories but come up blank. "Nothing," I whisper.

The old man frowns, inching closer to his daughter. "What?" he asks her.

"Nothing," the girl repeats.

"He said something, I heard him—"

"That's what he said, Papa. Nothing."

The old man eyes me curiously through one able eye; the other is covered by a black patch. The many lines on his face augment with concern. "What is your name, lad?"

For the first time since I opened my eyes, I feel the cold sweat of fear seep from my skin. "I don't know."

"The injury on his head," the girl whispers to her father.

The man nods. "It might only be a temporary condition." He turns his attention back to me. "The coin around your neck has the name Connor inscribed on it. Does that sound familiar?"

"No," I answer, reaching for the silver coin.

"Papa, we should let him rest. Maybe he'll remember when he's feeling better," the girl says, getting to her feet and pulling the old man along with her.

"I'll bring you some water," she says as they depart.

Between the pain and my all-consuming confusion, all I can do is wait. I close my eyes. The image of a girl appears. A girl with long, blond curls that drape to the waist of her plain, white dress. I feel like I know her, but I don't recognize her. Is this a memory? Then a crimson stain appears at the side of her abdomen. It blooms like a flower on the fabric of her dress. Blood. I watch, helpless, as the bleeding spreads. She looks me in the eye and utters two words.

"Save me."

About The Author

Samantha Gillespie is a creative, helpless romantic who was born in Mexico, where she grew up with her family until they returned to the States at age eleven. An avid reader from a young age, Samantha finally gave into her passion for writing, making her debut with *The Kingdom Within*.

Samantha considered pursuing a degree in English Literature while in college but despite her family and friend's encouragement, she opted for a more practical career in Business. Now, with the publication of her first book under her belt, she occasionally hits herself on the head for it. Samantha currently lives in Houston, TX with her husband, David, and their pets, Foxi, Moomy & Squeaky.

CONNECT WITH THE KINGDOM WITHIN

Website: www.thekingdomwithinseries.com
Facebook: www.facebook.com/tkwseries
Goodreads: www.goodreads.com/book/show/22875768-the-
               kingdom-within
Twitter: @ S_gillespie_

View the Book Trailer at:
www.youtu.be/OhXVILEzHjE